MW00810568

GOTTA GO TO COME BACK

ABBY GEORGE BOOK 2

ANNE KEMP

DAY ONE

"How did you get my address?"

Abby George was not a happy person. Well, at least not at the moment. Her normal laid-back demeanor had been swept away mere moments ago when a flower delivery man had paid a visit to her apartment in North Hollywood, knocking ever so hesitantly on her door marked #5.

For someone who had deplaned in L.A. a little more than twelve hours ago, Abby -- surrounded by boxes and brown wrapping paper -- was frighteningly ahead of the game. Making the decision to stay on the island of St. Kitts and run her family's bed-and-breakfast had felt like the right choice. It was one she felt she needed to make, because for the last few years her life had been flipped upside down.

Just a few months ago she had been laid off from her job as an executive coordinator and head of VIP relations for a local corporation run by CEO Guy. Devastated and in shock, she ended up in St. Kitts because her sister, Leigh, wanted her there. Leigh, Abby's perfect older sister, the one who never did wrong, needed her help. Turned out she was hiding an inn, secrets for their father, and a half-brother Abby never knew existed.

To think you weren't even in my life a few months ago, Abby thought to herself as she watched Ben sorting through her kitchen items as they organized boxes to be packed away in storage, dropped at Goodwill or shipped to St. Kitts. Since landing that morning, Abby had swept Ben into her flurry of activity. They had less than a week to pack up her place, see some sights for Ben's sake (it was his spring break, after all) and get back to the island for the first day of the last half of his final semester.

Standing in her kitchen, pacing wildly like a caged animal, taking in the gorgeous bouquet that was stuffed full of pink tulips, yellow daisies, white calla lilies, purple hyacinths and Queen Anne's lace, Abby confronted the person on the other end of the line.

"You're not answering me. I can hear you breathing, so I know you're there." Abby pursed her lips together and took a deep yoga breath, in through the nose, out through the mouth. She aimed for a quiet expulsion of slow breath, instead having it erupt like a volcano into the phone's mouthpiece. "J. D.! I am being quite serious. How did you get my address?"

If Abby could have placed a bet, she was willing to let it ride that J. D. was sitting on a balcony at the Frigate

Beach Hotel overlooking the Caribbean, smiling wickedly.

She stood in silent defiance and waited. She wanted him to explain how he had found her home when she had left suddenly from the island, avoiding him at all costs. During her time on St. Kitts, J. D. had appeared in her world almost as if by chance. First as a possible suitor, then as a conflict of interest. Not only did he want to win Abby but also he wanted to buy La Cantina, the inn she'd discovered had been left to her, her half-brother, Ben, and sister, Leigh, by their father. J. D.'s family owned Rhys Industries, a hotel group that had been slowly but steadily moving into the Caribbean islands, buying up smaller properties and converting them to Rhys Hotel Properties. They had been positioning themselves for the past few years to take over smaller hotels, revolutionizing how middle- to upper-income families vacationed much in the way Ace Hotels had done with its chain.

So she waited. She waited for him to talk, listening to him breathe, thinking about the last time he had kissed her on the front porch of the inn. She hadn't known who he was, exactly, nor had he known anything about her. And even though she had made a promise to Andrew to give their relationship a chance, she still could not stop thinking about J.D.'s lips on hers that day.

Andrew Van Dyk and J.D. Rhys. Two such different men. Andrew was nine years younger than Abby and worked for the Rhys family, while J.D. was much closer to her age, if anything just a few years older. Andrew, an old friend of Ben's, was visiting during a work trip when he and Abby were introduced. It wasn't quite love at first sight, but she couldn't deny that she felt something for Andrew.

At last, the voice spoke up on the other end.

"You have a terrible way of saying thank you."

Abby stomped her foot. Unfortunately she didn't pay attention to what she was stomping and she stomped directly on a small bread plate by her feet, shattering it into a million pieces. Irritated, she retorted into her cell, "Thank you? You stalk me and I'm supposed to say 'thank you'? Do you think Jodie Foster sent John Hinckley, Jr., a thank-you note?"

There was a pause followed by a low, throaty chuckle. Abby could have sworn he was growling seductively into the phone. "Abby, I could hardly be considered a stalker. I heard you had left and wanted you to know I was thinking of you. Did you not get the card that was supposed to come with the flowers?"

"Ah." Abby glanced at the small card in her hands. It was the size of a business card with a picture of yellow roses in the corner. Scribbled across the center of the page was a simple "Thinking of you every day, J.D."

"I did get the card, so yes. I now know you're thinking of me."

More silence. Abby was beginning to feel that maybe she was the jerk in this situation but yet she couldn't forget what she did know about J. D.

"Since you won't speak up, I will." Abby stepped

gingerly over Ben's head to navigate her way out of the kitchen and into the living room. She needed a moment to sit down and deal with this. "You sent Andrew back to London on purpose once you figured out we were together, didn't you?"

Silence.

"Okay. I'm obviously on to something. Maybe these flowers are your way of saying 'I'm sorry' because of your actions. And the fact that you all but threatened me that you were still going to pursue buying La Cantina. Is that it?"

"Abby, if you think I'm supposed to apologize to you then I have to say, you're completely correct."

"What!" Abby was prepared to attack when the words he uttered slowly began to sink in. "Wait. I'm right?"

"You are."

That was painless, she thought.

"Do you mind filling in some of the gaps for me please, J.D.?"

There was a heavy sigh on the other end. Abby could see him in her mind's eye: He was standing facing the sea, hanging his head low as he looked down over Ricky's Beach Bar and Café, a cold bottle of Carib in his hand.

"Okay, Abby. I figured it out when he was talking so much about you. I knew that you and the Abby he spoke of were one and the same. So yes, I wanted to get him back to London as soon as I could. I thought my time with you would be brief, since I was about to buy the inn from your sister. I thought you'd be leaving."

5

Abby grinned into her iPhone. "Guess we surprised you when we said we weren't selling?"

Abby could hear his smile as he answered. "Yes, you did. I wasn't expecting that."

"Good. Glad I had some element of surprise."

"Bravo. Personally, I love surprises. However, I've been picking up the pieces of that debacle since our meeting."

"So I got you in trouble with Daddy?" Abby couldn't help it. She had to be a little snarky. It was J.D., after all.

"He's not happy that I lost La Cantina. Apparently he thinks I'm too caught up with my island-hopping ways."

"Good for him. Someone needs to put you in your place." God, she loved to trade barbs with him. "What's he going to do? Ground you?"

J.D. made a sound like a balloon hissing as air was being let out of it. "No, he's actually sending my sister, Callie, here to work with me as we revamp Ricky's and the Frigate Beach Hotel. Which means I'm not going anywhere for a long time."

Abby wasn't sure if she should consider the last sentence a threat.

"Well, it sounds as if your dad just wants you to get your act together."

"He wants me to get La Cantina."

"It's no longer for sale."

"Everything has a price, Abby."

Abby's irritation was beginning to rise again. She was staring at Ben, watching as he wrapped her wineglasses, carefully and gently, resting them in their new cardboard homes. This reminded her there was wine for the drinking. She stood up, took a glass from Ben's grasp and headed to her wine cabinet. As J.D. continued, she opened a nice bottle of pinot noir and poured a glass for Ben and herself.

She took a hearty swig before she launched her verbal stream.

"There's something you need to understand. First of all, La Cantina is not for sale, nor will it be at any point in the near future. Second of all, I am not for sale, nor is any member of my family, nor will we be at any point in the near future. Third of all, you sending Andrew back to London because you wanted him out of the way? That was absolutely insane. I'm going to ask that you don't ever do that again. Please don't mess with his life. You cannot just send someone away because it suits you!"

"I'm his boss, Abby. If I need him to be somewhere at a moment's notice, he's going to have to go." J.D. was thoughtful as he continued, "However, I mean it when I say I'm sorry that I did that."

Can I really believe you? Abby thought while sipping her wine, listening to his apology.

"You aren't sure if I'm sincere, are you?"

"No, I'm not." Abby sighed heavily as she cursed his clairvoyance. "I want to believe you, I really do."

"I can't make you, but I can send flowers until you're back. Then maybe you'll allow me to show you I can be sincere."

That did it. Abby's body flushed with heat as she pressed her lips together, pursing them tight. The memory of his hand under her shirt, his fingertips tracing her back as he pressed her body close to his. She closed her eyes and willed her body to get a grip. She threw all of her concentration into refocusing her attention to their call so she could get off the phone. She knew she needed to disconnect and get back to packing, but now her head was filled with her dangerous island-tryst fantasies. Not something she needed to have when Andrew was a continent away and she was truly devoting herself to him.

Wasn't she?

Abby could feel her stomach turning. If there was one thing she didn't need to enter her world right now it was self-doubt. Too many important decisions had been made in the last few months to turn back now, right? She was leaving L.A., taking up running La Cantina and starting fresh on St. Kitts. And she had promised Andrew she would give a relationship with him a shot, even with the distance. So she was feeling a touch guilty and confused about this call and the flowers.

She knew she had to hang up, but before she was able to end the call, J.D. interrupted her.

"I can tell you have a lot on your plate, Abby. I didn't mean to bother you, I just wanted a chance to apologize and to let you know that I was thinking of you."

Abby swallowed the small lump that was in her throat.

"Apology accepted. And thank you, the flowers are gorgeous."

"Good. And it was Ziggy."

"Ziggy?"

"He told me where you'd be for the next week with Ben. I told him I needed to send you some information on tourism for the island."

Abby couldn't help the smile that curled the ends of her lips upward. "You are a piece of work, you know that?"

"I really wanted to get my point across."

Abby didn't know what to say, so she kept her mouth shut in fear that she would add fuel to his fire if she engaged him any longer. The silence over the airwaves was a bit heavy for her liking and Abby could sense the energy and mood had shifted between them.

"I'm going to go. Take care, J.D."

"I'll see you soon, Abby. Travel safe."

Abby hit the "End" button on her iPhone and turned to her half-brother.

"Seriously, Ben, why the hell is he so persistent?"

Ben laughed at her, shaking his head as he taped one box closed, scribbling in black magic marker on the top of the old cardboard box, "Kitchen: Glassware."

"Take it as a compliment Abby," Ben answered in his thick British accent. "He obviously wants to win you over."

Abby rolled her eyes and took a slow sip out of her wineglass. "I know, and that's the problem, Ben. He wants to win, not just win me over. And it's not just me. He wants to win anything. He wants to win La Cantina." She got up and walked in to the kitchen and sat on the floor next to her brother. "What if he does? Win the inn and take it from me? Then what do I do?"

"Abby, you can't think like that. You can't let him get into your head and have you doubt yourself."

"I know." Abby sat back against the old yellow refrigerator, letting her head rest on its cool, textured surface. "I also don't want Andrew getting caught in all of this. No matter what, he's your friend. I can't have anything that happens between him and me or that results because of J.D. being a pain in the ass affect your relationship with him." She scrunched her nose up as if she smelled something bad. "Nope, I just won't have it."

Ben folded from his crouched position over the boxes into a sitting position and scooted back against the wall opposite Abby.

"Trust me, I won't let it happen either. But it helps to hear that you feel the same way." He took a frat-boy swig of the wine. "Not everyone would think like that, Abs. It's sweet of you to make sure I'm going to be happy dealing with your situation."

"There I go," she giggled. "Always the assistant."

As if on cue, Abby's phone began chiming with the ringtone of a guitar strumming. It was Leigh, checking in on the pair.

"Hey, you! You're on speaker with the Ben and Abby show."

"At least you sound chipper." Leigh's voice was scratchy. Abby could tell she'd been smoking more when her voice was raspy like this.

"I'm as chipper as you are when you light your after-work smoke and take the first sip of your after-work

GOTTA GO TO COME BACK

scotch," she teased. Thankfully, Leigh had been in a good mood lately, so the sisters were getting along and had formed a more united front since the whole St. Kitts excursion.

"I take it you got the flowers?"

"Did everyone get the memo but me?"

"Seems Mr. Rhys tricked our Ziggy, didn't he?" Leigh snickered on the other end. "Actually, Maria was giving him hell for telling J.D. your address in L.A. I happened to call right when she was in the middle of giving him a good 'what for,' as she said."

Abby had to admit that J.D. was good. Sneaky, but good at being sneaky. "Yes, he did. Poor Ziggy. I really don't blame him. I do know I will never trust him with any major secrets, though."

Maria, an old family friend, had helped take care of the inn for many years. Ziggy, Maria's husband, was originally from St. Kitts and helped out on the property as needed while operating a taxicab business on the side. These two were as polar opposite as you could get, making Abby believe that opposites really do attract.

"So, how's it going in L.A.? You and Ben getting settled?"

Abby waved her hand in his direction. "I'll let Ben answer that one."

"Settled?" Ben chortled. "Leigh, this place is a disaster. We've succeeded in turning it upside down."

"But you'll be done by the end of the week?"

Abby and Ben caught each other's eyes and nodded in

firm agreement. "Yes. I think we'll have it all wrapped up by then. Hopefully with a day to spare to actually relax before we fly out."

"Excellent. Well, I gave Maria the go-ahead on the marketing plan you two have been firming up. Once you have a finished product, may I take a last scan over it before you go live with it?"

Abby's smile was infectious as it lit the room. "Of course! I'm so glad you like it. I think that starting the blog about the inn and doing a social media campaign is a great way for us to get the word out about La Cantina without diving into any funds at the moment. Ben's actually going to set up a Twitter account for the inn that we can use to promote specials and run discounts and contests."

"Did Abby tell you about the Rum Punch Happy Hour we're starting?" Ben asked as he stretched his arm in Abby's direction, holding out his wineglass, asking silently for more. "I think on Fridays we're going to attempt some steel drums around the pool with rum punch and snacks."

"It's going to be a 'get to know you' happy hour as well, so our guests can all mingle and get to know one another and all of us at the property."

"I loved it. I told Maria it was one of the best ideas I'd heard. I also liked the idea of group dinner outings with the guests to restaurants and participating in activities together, like the hikes and canopy tours in the rainforest." Leigh's voice was proud. "Smart girl, Abs."

"We're creating a mini-community." She was beaming with pride. "A Caribbean subculture, if you will."

Leigh was pleased. "I knew you could do this. I'm proud of you. This is such a big risk and change for you." Leigh's voice had gotten a bit softer. "You really do inspire me, Abby. Right when I think the world has knocked you down for the last time and you may not get up, you do."

"I really don't know what to say, Leigh."

"Say nothing. Just keep La Cantina up and running and see your commitment through, okay?"

Abby smiled and nodded as she poured herself some wine from the bottle. "You got it. I'm going to do all of you proud."

"Well, you'd better. If not, I can still pop your air mattress," Ben teased.

"That or your cats will."

Before the pair could lapse into their playful bickering, Abby said her good-byes. "Leigh, I'll be in touch. We'll get wrapped up here and head back at the end of the week. And thank you for taking such good care of the place and for having Will bring Giles down for me!"

Right before Abby and Ben had left for L.A., Leigh's son Will had come to the island to meet his uncle, deliver Abby's cat, Giles, and spend some time on the island. The trio had spent a few fun days together before Abby had to corral the two boys and get everyone to L.A. for work and school.

"I think you may have secured an intern for the summer if you'll have him."

Abby giggled at the thought. "An intern, huh? You know what, since he's studying business and has a good head for marketing and sales, I'll take him!"

"Deal. Okay, you two." Leigh's tone had picked up its usual frantic pace as she wrapped up their call. "Time to go. Good luck and I'll check in with you later this week."

Abby held up her hand and counted down with her fingers, "3-2-1," with Ben.

"We love you!"

Leigh's laugh filled the room. "Okay, love you weirdos. 'Bye!"

As the call disconnected, Abby stood up. "I think we have a few more boxes in the kitchen. Do you mind wrapping them up while I take pictures of the furniture I'm going to sell so I can get it up online? I'd love to get the biggest pieces out of here today or tomorrow if I can."

Ben nodded as he hauled himself back into a crouching position over a new box all primed and ready to be stuffed full with more of Abby's things. "You got it."

Abby stood on her tiptoes, using her hand as she felt along the top of her kitchen cabinets, searching for her camera. She had a knack for hiding things in unusual places, and this was one of them. She knew she had struck gold when her fingers hit the cool metal exterior of her small Canon PowerShot. She added an extra inch to her length by stretching and rising up on her tiptoes with a precision that would rival any prima ballerina's, and grabbed her camera.

"If we can get a huge majority of this stuff organized

today and tomorrow, I'm taking you out to dinner tomorrow night." She knew she had to show Ben a good time amid all of the crazy-making packing while they were in L.A.

Ben's green eyes lit up. "That'd be great, Abs. Thank you."

"It's the least I can do since you're helping me and because I'm just ordering us a cheap pizza for dinner tonight." She grinned.

Making her way into the living room, Abby pulled her long chestnut mane back into a tight ponytail as she took one last look at her living room in its put-together entirety. Within a few hours, she and Ben would have this place torn up and boxed, ready to be closed up for good. She could feel a sad thud in her chest as she reflected on the happy times she and Matt had shared there in the years prior.

Matt was Abby's ex-fiancé. Thanks to him cheating on her and then leaving her, she had been left broke and broken-hearted by this man. She had figured with Matt it was what love was supposed to be like; it was comfortable, there were days that she wanted to kill him, but no matter what she was happy to be a part of his life and have him be a part of hers. She had loved him with all of her heart. But sometimes, she couldn't deny that in the back of her head there was a nagging, a voice that questioned if she was with him for the right reason, as if she was just settling for him and not settling down. Not that it mattered, because when he left her for the girl that recorded stats for his softball team, she had turned off her emotions to him as soon as she was able to move past it. In fact, she had managed to turn off her emotions to any man, for the most part.

At least she'd thought so.

Then she'd met Andrew. Thinking of him, she raised her arm to admire the beautiful charm bracelet he had given her a few weeks ago, before he flew back to London. The bracelet was silver, delicate links with two charms attached to it: one charm was designed as twin palms growing from the same trunk and boasting an emerald, the other a heart with a ruby set inside. She played with the small charms, letting them balance delicately on her fingertips as she smiled at the memory of his excitement when he'd presented her with the bracelet. He truly was a sweetheart. One of a kind. And she was lucky to have met him.

Snapping out of her daydream, Abby clapped her hands together to bring herself back to reality. Turning on the camera, she took aim at her old couch and her beloved coffee table and began clicking away.

DAY TWO

"You seriously want to keep this?"

Abby looked at the small trophy Ben was holding and grinned. "If I'm not mistaken, that would be from the Watermelon Eatin' Contest . . . correct?"

"Yes, you hillbilly, it is." He shook his head as he placed it into her outstretched hand. "And don't think I didn't notice it says "eatin'" and not "eating."

Abby held the trophy carefully and smiled. "This thing has gone with me everywhere. Dad and Mom took me to this county fair when I was little; I think we were vacationing in Virginia near Hampton Roads. When we got there, I saw all of these colorful signs for the 'Dill Pickle Eatin' Contest' and the 'Hot Dog Eatin' Contest.' Then I saw the sign for the Watermelon Eatin' Contest. I ended up eating half of one in less than a minute. Seeds and all." Abby grinned at the memory.

"Don't you mean eatin'?"

"Shut up!" Abby chucked some packing paper in Ben's direction. "It's not like I was coordinated enough for team sports."

Ben swatted at Abby playfully, then took the trophy back, wrapped it carefully and placed it aside in her "coming with me" box. "Anything else we need to add to this right now?"

"No, I wrapped my Great Gatsby book and put it in there earlier. I'll add some photos and some other little things I want to bring as we go."

The world outside Abby's little apartment was dark and cloaked in silence as the night snuck in. Abby was turning on lights so they could see better, when she glanced at her watch, realizing it was almost dinnertime. "Poor Ben! Two days of packing and seeing the inside of my place. Not a fun way to take in L.A."

Ben just shrugged his shoulders. "It's okay."

"No, it really isn't." Abby closed the box she was working on and stood up. "Let's go."

Ben shot her a questioning look. "Why?"

Abby walked over to her brother and pulled on his arm. "Because, what kind of sister would I be if I didn't get us out of here for dinner at least once? It's your spring break, Ben."

As Abby grabbed his arm, Ben rose with the motion, as if she were dragging him along. As soon as she let go, he grabbed his jacket and baseball hat and began marching to the door.

"Ben?"

Ben turned and clapped his hands at his sister. "Chop, chop, Abs. I'm starving. Let's go!"

THE INSIDE OF STUDIO CITY SUSHI WAS PACKED WITH after-work meetings, dates and the occasional celebrity sitting at one of the tables. SC Sushi, as the neighborhood crowd called it, was a hidden gem in the Valley that only locals and diehard sushi fans knew about. This was a small miracle considering that this part of L.A. was known for having the most sushi restaurants per capita this side of Tokyo.

Abby's heart sank when they entered as she realized the wait could take forever. She began to back out of the restaurant so she and Ben could reassess their dinner plans. But the sinking feeling soon turned to elation as a familiar voice called out to her from behind the host stand.

"Abby George! Dinner for two? Or one tonight?"

Surprised, Abby turned to see Lin, one of the owners of SC Sushi, grinning at her from behind the counter.

"Lin! How are you?"

Lin came around from behind her stand and wrapped her tiny arms around Abby, pulling her tight as old friends do.

"So good, Abby. We've been busy. Remember the dinner menu I told you about?"

"The idea you had for hourly specials?"

"That's the one! Ever since the recession, it's been one

ANNE KEMP

of the most popular menus we've ever had. I still have you to thank for helping us with the marketing for that!" Lin smiled at her old patron. "Where have you been? We've missed you here."

"Traveling, Lin. Just been gone a lot lately." She looked around the tiny restaurant and smiled, thinking back to all of the nights she'd spent here, reading a book, or coming on dates, then dinners out with Matt. "I've missed you guys, too." Abby turned to Ben. "Ben, this is Lin, one of the owners. I was a regular here for many years."

"More than a regular. Abby would help us evaluate and revamp our marketing and menus every few months to keep prices affordable and our customers happy." Lin looked Ben up and down, as if taking in a prized Monet at the Smithsonian. "Ben. Who are you?"

Abby giggled. "Lin, Ben is my brother. He's here helping me pack my place."

"Ben, so nice to meet you. I never knew you had a brother, Abby!"

Ben smiled at Lin and leaned in, whispering, "I never knew I had a sister, so we're kind of even."

Lin giggled flirtatiously with him as she grabbed two menus. "I always have a spot for your sister here, especially since I need her to tell me why she's packing!"

Lin began a zigzag through the throng of people clustered together with an ease that rivaled an Indy driver on a crowded track. Abby and Ben followed her to a small table tucked in the back corner, out of the way of the hustle and bustle of the after-work congregation.

As she squeezed into her seat, settling in for her meal, Abby took Lin's hand. "Packing to move, Lin. Looks like I'm going to run an inn in the Caribbean."

Lin's eyes widened with surprise and excitement. "The Caribbean? In charge of an inn?" She nodded her head in full approval. "Congratulations!" Then she leaned into Ben's ear and stage-whispered, "Make sure you give me the card so I can come visit. You can show me around, okay?"

And with a wiggle of her eyebrows and blowing a kiss in the air, Lin was off, leaving Ben shaking his head in disbelief.

"And I thought St. Kitts had characters," he whispered across the table.

Abby laughed as she scanned the menu. "Want me to do the ordering?"

Ben acquiesced as the waitress approached the table. She placed a large bottle of Tsingtao on the table with two glasses, followed by a small pitcher in the shape of a bamboo stalk filled with sake for them.

"Compliments of the house." She smiled at the pair as she poured their drinks and scribbled down their order.

"Cheers." Ben held his beer glass in the air as he toasted Abby. "To your move and new life."

"Here's to that!" Abby laughed as they clinked their glasses against each other and took a drink. It was a drink she almost choked on as she was throwing it down.

As she was taking her swig, Abby's gaze had been averted to a couple at the front door, the guy with his arm wrapped around his glowing girlfriend's waist. She was grinning an electric smile, perfect white teeth showing, beaming up at him and standing on her tiptoes to kiss his lips. Abby drank in his movements as he leaned over Lin's desk, kissing her on the cheek and pulling the tiny blonde fairy closer to his body. Anyone could see they were a couple in love and happy to share with the world their love of each other. The movements were hauntingly familiar, ones she remembered participating in all too well in the not-so-distant past. Abby could feel her world spinning just a little with a nervous rush of adrenaline coursing through her veins at the speed of a locomotive.

She could feel the color drain from her face as Lin caught her eye over Matt's shoulder, making silent eye contact, as if asking permission to let him come in. Abby gulped, swallowing hard over the lump in her throat, and nodded.

"Abby, what just happened?" Ben's face was placid and calm but his tone was worried.

She took a big breath and sat up straight and smiled. "Matt, my ex. He just walked in with his girlfriend."

Ben started to turn around.

"No! Don't turn around," she said through gritted teeth. "Don't. Move."

He cocked his head to the side. "Why the hell are you so worried?"

"Why? Because he left me, Ben. For her. He cheated

on me, with her." Abby looked down at the table and felt all of the old emotions she thought had gone now come back to haunt her. "God, he broke my heart, Ben."

Ben leaned over the table, vying for attention. "Hey, you stop this pity party right now. You don't do that."

Abby looked up at her brother and smiled. "I know, but how do you make the heart forget? Make my mind forget? Hell, make my ego forget?"

He shrugged, taking a long pull on his beer. "You just do. Plus, you're leaving here, so screw it. And there's Andrew." Ben put down his beer glass and picked up the sake cup, taking his shot and pounding it back. "Oh, and J.D. Can't forget about him, too."

Abby rolled her eyes as Ben tossed back another sake. "Really? You need to bring that up right now? And don't go getting all hammered, mister. Throwing up sushi sucks."

"I'm a college student, Abby, I'm supposed to drink like this."

Abby shook her head and allowed her eyes to wander back over to the front door once more. Matt and Stats Girl were nowhere in sight.

Breathing a sigh of relief, she sat back in her chair. "Maybe they left."

"Stop being neurotic and relax, please," Ben said as he reached across the table and topped off her Tsingtao for her. "He screwed up, right? So you have nothing to worry about. For Pete's sake, Abs, hold your head high and stop being such a div."

Abby curled her upper lip in mock horror. "Div? And what, pray tell, did I do to deserve that putdown?"

"Do you even know what it means?"

She started to nod, changing course and shaking her head, laughing. "Of course not. What the hell is a div?"

"It's British slang for idiot. You're defining 'div' at the moment." Ben grabbed his sake cup and threw another back as he kept going. "You're making a big deal outta nowt, Abs."

"And you're using more slang than I've ever heard." She reached over and picked up the bamboo pitcher housing what was left of the sake and found it alarmingly empty. "Well, someone needs to let off some steam. Should I order another?"

Ben grinned, pushing the bamboo pitcher and Tsingtao bottle to the edge of the table, making it easier for a server to clear.

"I'm on spring break and I think we need a little more of both. You need to keep up."

"Ha. We know how well that goes for me."

Before she could go on, the waitress was back, already with another round in each hand. Abby and Ben looked at each other, confused, since they hadn't ordered.

"This is from Lin, Abby. She wanted me to tell you she was sorry."

"Sorry?" Abby squinted her eyes in confusion. "For what?"

Answering her own question, she looked up to see Lin making her way through the crowd and walking toward her table wearing a nervous expression. Her eyes darted to the table next to Abby. Still confused, Abby looked at the table, and saw it was free, a small two-top that was almost on top of the table where she and Ben sat. She looked back at Lin, not understanding, mouthing "What?" just as Lin popped out of the crowd of people milling about with her guests following suit.

It was then that she realized Lin was sorry because Abby was about to share a meal with Matt and Stats Girl. She took the sake cup that Ben held out to her and threw it down her throat as she grabbed her beer and took a huge swig.

Dinner was about to get interesting.

"Abby?"

Forcing a smile (after receiving a kick under the table from Ben, who was thoroughly amused), Abby looked up, feigning surprise.

"Matt! Wow, this is a surprise. What brings you here?"

The pair had stopped awkwardly in the middle of the crowded restaurant, frozen in place. Abby could smell the fear Stats Girl was reeking as she averted her eyes to every part of the room except toward Abby.

"It was actually Ann-Marie's idea. She surprised me with a reservation here tonight. She knew I used to come here . . ."

He trailed off as Lin began to scoot them into their table. "Sit, sit. Sorry you need to be on top of one another. I'll send over some more drinks. Some food." And with that, Lin scurried away. Probably in fear I may spin out like a whirling dervish, Abby thought.

"I guess this is dinner, then," Abby said with resignation as she glanced around the restaurant, noting there weren't any other tables to be had. She looked at Ben and mouthed, "This is awesome."

Ben couldn't suppress his laughter any longer. From the moment they had realized Matt was on his way over, he had done his best, but it was too much now as the sake and beer began to take over. He slapped his hand down on the table and leaned over and tapped Abby on the tip of her nose with his left forefinger, slurring, "You are awesome."

He then turned his attention to their accidental dinner companions. "Hello, mates. So," he began, wagging his finger and nodding his head, "you must be Matt. Heard about you. But you" -- Ben then turned his boyish charm in Ann-Marie's direction -- "I only know a wee-tiny bit about."

Still looking nervous and shaken, Ann-Marie mustered a smile while answering Ben. Her voice was soft and quiet, almost a whisper. "I'm Ann-Marie. And you are?"

"Ben. Nice to meet you both. So . . . how was your day, dear?"

Abby's jaw dropped as she realized Ben was heading at top speed into really-freaking-drunk territory. She looked around for the waitress, hoping to add some pot stickers and rice to their order to help soak up some of the booze before he got really out of hand.

Matt turned to Abby, albeit nervously, and held up his hands. "Look, this is going to be weird. Should we go?"

Abby bit her lower lip, feeling the pain but knowing if she didn't bite it she might start speaking. Instead of answering, she slowly shook her head. It was a move that Ben took as a bit too passive-aggressive, apparently, so he waged on.

"Whaaat?" He threw his hand to his mouth in mock surprise, a funny and flamboyant move that normally would have made Abby laugh but this time only instilled in her a bit of horror. "Why would you want to go?"

"Ben,"Abby hissed under her breath at her brother, willing his lips sealed shut.

"I'm being serious. Maybe my new friend, Ann-Marie, can tell me a bit about why the question would even come up." Ben's eyes were drunkenly sparkling as he turned to his right and leaned in closer to the tiny blonde sitting next to him. "Do you know?"

Thankfully, they were all saved from any more awkwardness for the time being, as the waitress showed up with Abby and Ben's dinner. Breathing a sigh of relief, Abby helped organize the plates on the table, ordered the rice and pot stickers for Ben, and insisted he dig in imme-diately, more in an effort to shut him up than to feed him into sobriety. Ben had started to open his mouth again, but a quick swift kick from Abby under the table and a not-so-thrilled glare made him think twice. Instead, grin-ning at his sister in a playful, drunken manner, he began eating.

As she mixed her soy sauce with her wasabi, Abby found herself wishing she could telepathically tell Ben to shut up, but instead just prayed he would stay quiet for the rest of the meal.

Pushing her baked crab roll around in her soy sauce concoction, Abby couldn't help but sneak glances at Matt and Ann-Marie. This honestly wouldn't sting so much if he hadn't been cheating on me with her, she thought to herself as she attempted to swallow her bite. Just the mere reminder that the couple sitting next to her was part of her "old" life was enough to send a chill over her body. Abby just couldn't discern if she was shuddering because of the hurt they had caused or because she felt she owed them a thank-you because her life had changed immensely since them.

Deciding on the latter, Abby realized she just needed to make peace with the situation. Thank God we never got married or had kids. I never would have left L.A., met Andrew, began a new life . . . I might never have met Ben. That secret could have stayed buried. Abby was distractedly and protectively watching her brother as he wolfed down his food. Every now and then he would grin lopsidedly at her, throwing the occasional toast in the air with his sake cup. Yes, Abby hated to admit it, but Matt cheating on her was right up there with getting laid off; it was truly a good thing. But why does it still sting so badly?

To her chagrin, Ben had engaged Ann-Marie in conversation again.

"So, Ann-Marie, why did you two decide to come here tonight? Any fun reason?" he baited.

Ann-Marie flashed her megawatt million-dollar smile, batted her eyelashes at Ben and answered, "Actually, we're celebrating our anniversary."

Ben clapped his hands together in mock happiness, ignoring the glare seething from Abby's side of the table. "Really! Which one? Six months? Nine?"

Oblivious to his tone, Ann-Marie grabbed Matt's hand across their table. "A year and a half," she proclaimed proudly, grinning lovingly at her man.

Abby took a bite of her food, calculating the time frame in her head. Ben was about to ramble on some more bullshit, but she held up a chopstick, speaking with her mouth full.

"How long, Ann-Marie?"

Abby could see Matt cringe out of the corner of her eye as her question hit its mark.

"A year and a half."

Abby swallowed her food and took a swig of sake. "Huh. That's pretty interesting. Considering Matt and I broke up just about a year ago, give or take a month . . . right, Matt?"

She turned to her ex only to be met with a downcast look and eyes that would not meet hers.

You asshole.

Unreal. So the whole thing had gone on longer than she had thought. She looked at the wooden chopstick in her hand and was almost gleeful at the thought that she had the proper tool in case she wanted to stake one of them in the heart at this moment.

Pondering this, Abby popped the last bite of her baked crab roll into her mouth. Instead of it landing on her tongue for her to savor and enjoy its delicious crab, mayo and soy-paper goodness, her sushi launched itself to the back of her throat and stayed there. She paused and gave a silent cough, attempting to force it down by chasing it with a swig of Ben's sake. Instead, she found that it wasn't going anywhere. As her heart began to race and her throat began to hurt, Abby realized in her panic that she was choking on her food.

Abby's eyes were wild with fear and embarrassment as she kicked Ben under the table. He begrudgingly looked up at her, mouthing "What?" as she pointed at her throat, coughing in spurts and tapping the table with her other hand. Ben was oblivious to the international charade for "I'm choking."

"Too much wasabi?" he asked.

You have got to be kidding me! Abby continued to point, except now she was leaning her stomach forward on the table, trying to find a spot where she could administer the Heimlich maneuver on herself. All the times I thought I'd be alone and choke and have to save myself, she thought. Now, here I am in a crowed restaurant and it's still up to me!

It was Matt who noticed the commotion next to him.

"Abs? You okay? Shit, Abby, stand up!"

In one quick move, Matt grabbed Abby by her arm

and pulled her up, spinning her around so her back was pressed to his chest. He threw his arms around her and delivered a few quick pumps from his interlaced fists to her abdomen, going in and up. On his third thrust, the crab roll that was lodged in her throat came flying out. Right in front of Ann-Marie, who promptly screamed and threw herself backward in her chair.

Abby was vaguely aware of the slow flush beginning to creep up into her cheeks as she watched Ben soothing Ann-Marie and cleaning up her food, with Lin running over to help and several patrons leaning in and coming over asking if she needed anything. It was all very surreal and very embarrassing. She was, however, more than aware that Matt still had his arms around her, almost holding her like the old days, except in the old days he had never saved her from choking on her food.

"You're shaking. Can I get you anything?" Matt had released her and was handing her over to Ben, now that Ann-Marie had been calmed down.

She shook her head. "No, I think I just need to take a minute."

Abby murmured "Thank you" to the small crowd who had gathered, expressing their concern, and made a beeline for the front door. All she could see right now was getting out.

As she pushed through the door, a blast of cool air hit her face and she closed her eyes and took a big breath. She searched for a spot in the parking lot where she could sit on the curb for a moment and then sank to the ground, hugging her knees and resting her head on them.

"That was close."

She didn't have to look up to know that it was Matt who had followed her out.

"I do know how to make dinner interesting, don't I?" Her voice was raspy as she sighed into her jeans.

She could feel Matt suppressing his laughter as he sat next to her. "You always knew how to get a party started, Abby. Leave it to you to fire up a doozy tonight."

Lifting her head, she smiled at her ex. "Well, it's been a while, Matt. I needed to know I still had it."

They exchanged a smile as Abby stretched her legs out and sat up a little straighter. Even though her stomach was still reeling from the previous moment, she had to address the ache in her heart.

"A year and a half, Matt? Really?"

"I'm sorry." She could hear the sadness in his voice. "I should have told you, but when we were breaking up there was so much pain happening, I honestly didn't want to prolong it any more. I had hurt you enough. Did you really want to know at that point how long?"

He had a point, but Abby could still feel the sting. "I don't know, Matt. I don't know because I was never given the chance to know that information. But I do now, and honestly . . . I feel embarrassed and irritated."

She ran her fingers through her hair, pulling it off her face and over one shoulder. It really doesn't matter anymore, she thought. I need to let the matter go.

"Of all the places for us to run into each other," she began.

"I can't believe we ended up sitting next to each other."

She shook her head, but smiled in his direction. "I'm still mad at you, ya know. Not as much as I was. But I'm still mad."

Matt looked down at the pavement, trying to hide the guilty expression creeping across his features.

"I don't blame you. I handled it all wrong." He sighed. "If I could do it all over again differently, I would."

"It's actually good that it happened. We were stuck, in a rut or whatever. It just sucked that you cheated." She rotated her body where she sat and turned to face him, reaching out and angling him so he faced her. "We were planning a wedding, Matt. To be honest, the worst part was that you left me holding the bag."

The emotion Matt felt wore on his features, dragging down the corners of his mouth and cloaking his eyes in sadness. "I know. I actually would like to talk to you about that. I think I owe you some help in that department."

She waited expectantly for an explanation. "What department?"

"The financial one, Abs. I was a jerk."

Abby was shocked. "I'd really like that. If you could help me with some of the money I used, that would be great."

He nodded, his gaze still on the ground, not meeting hers. "I fucked up. Karma can be a bitch, but you never were." He slowly brought his eyes up to meet hers. "Hey, I like your date. He seems funny."

Abby was nodding her head absentmindedly until she realized he meant Ben.

"Ben? My date? Oh, no. Matt, Ben's my brother."

Matt's mouth dropped open. "Seriously?"

"Yeah," she chuckled. "Actually, a lot has happened since we last saw each other. I'm moving to the Caribbean. We're here packing up my place so I can take my things back down there. I'll be gone by the end of the week."

Matt sat taking in Abby's words. "Wow. You're not kidding that a lot's happened. What the hell, Abs?"

Abby chuckled and patted him on the back as she stood up. "I ask myself that all the time." She held out her hand to Matt, offering him help to stand up. "Come on, we should go back inside."

Matt took her hand and stood up, facing her. He put his hands on her shoulders and looked into her eyes.

"I'm sorry."

Abby nodded and swallowed the lump that was threatening to form in her throat. She managed to whisper "Thank you" before Matt enveloped her in his arms, hugging her.

"Funny we should run into each other, actually," he said as they pulled apart. "I found some of your things mixed in with one of my boxes the other day. Maybe I can bring it by?"

Abby nodded. "Of course. Anything important?"

He shrugged. "A few books, some clothes and some

files. So you're really leaving?"

"Yep," she answered, grinning up at him. "Crazy, huh?"

"I can't believe it. You always said you'd never leave L.A., Abs. You love it here."

It was Abby's turn to shrug her shoulders. "Things change, Matt. My tastes changed, my life changed and I found a world that makes me really happy down there." Abby looked through the window of the restaurant to where Ben and Ann-Marie were sitting. "This may sound hokey, but I've got purpose there."

"And what, pray tell, is that?"

"I'm going to be running an inn. Well, it's actually my family's, but it's mostly mine now. I'm in charge."

Her words landed on Matt with a thud. He was visibly taken aback as she told him. "You're running an inn? Your family has an inn?" He shook his head in disbelief. "My lord, Abby. Next thing I know, you're going to say you're running off with the King of England."

She giggled, and opened the door to head back inside. "Funny you should say that, because there is someone."

Matt's face registered faint surprise. "Really?"

"Well, he's not the King of England, but he's pretty fantastic." She held the door for him. "Come on. We can talk more at the table."

Matt smiled at his ex. "You're pretty fantastic, Abby George. You know that, right?"

Abby smiled to herself as they made their way through the restaurant and back to their seats. "You bet I do."

DAY THREE

"ABBY, DUCK!"

Unfortunately, the sound of Ben's voice didn't carry across the breeze as fast as either of them would have hoped. Those two words were the last ones Abby heard before she felt the equivalent of a frying pan hitting her on the side of her head.

Lying on the ground, she was hazily aware of Ben standing over her, of the throbbing she felt in her right temple and of the urge she had to throw up from the pain as it settled into the depths of her tummy like a hurricane swirling off the East Coast, dark and angry.

Her eyelids were fluttering as she tried to make sense of the past few moments, even the other parts of the day. Is it afternoon? Where am I? Abby's thoughts were a jumbled mess. Ben was crouching next to her, asking if she wanted to use him as support, and she felt the warmth of another body next to her, throwing her arm over his shoulders and scooping her up in the classic hero-rescues-the-heroine move. As her head flopped to rest on this person's shoulder, she remembered Matt was with them.

Wait. Matt?

Abby stiffened almost immediately, her eyes opening wide in panic. Fighting the crushing feeling happening inside her skull at the moment, Abby tried to twist around and slide out of Matt's grasp.

"What are you doing? Abby, quit wiggling. Let me get you in the shade." Matt's brow was sweaty and his face reflected his concern, although he had forced a smile so she wouldn't know.

She went to speak, but found the very act of opening her mouth made her feel like a marionette whose faux jaw had been cracked open. Every fiber of her being was aching, especially around her noggin, and Ben's repeated apologies weren't really helping.

"I don't know what I was thinking, Abs. But really, you weren't there a second ago." He was shaking his head and looking to Matt for support. "Really, she wasn't there."

Matt bent slowly next to the one tree in the parking lot that offered shade to shield the victim. Abby felt as if the world were spinning at top speed on its axis as he bent over to place her on the moist grass under the magnolia. She closed her eyes and listened to the two bicker back and forth over whether it was Abby's fault she had stood up at the wrong moment or theirs for throwing kitchen-ware around.

She could faintly remember the day: packing up her boxes with Ben, getting them into the truck, realizing on the way over to the storage unit they'd need help unloading. Okay, she thought. I called Matt for help? That makes no sense.

"Ben, she's fine."

"How do you know that, mate? Look at her." Ben was attempting to speak in a hushed tone, but his worry made his voice shake. "She's going to have a knot on the side of her head the size of a golf ball!"

Matt grinned. "Well, she's hardheaded. I doubt there's any serious damage done."

Speak for yourself, Abby thought. My head is cracking.

"Do you think she knows I did it?"

"I have a feeling she may," Matt replied. "Mostly 'cause you won't shut up."

Abby couldn't listen anymore. She sat up, taking them out of their misery.

"I'm fine. Stunned, but fine." She closed her eyes, took a deep breath and laid her head back down in the grass again. "What happened?"

The two men shifted awkwardly in their spots, eyeing each other, almost daring each other to go first.

"Seriously," Abby groaned from her prone position on the ground. "One of you needs to man up."

"We were doing what you told us to stop doing; throwing items you said were trash into the dumpster," Matt tentatively began.

"I told you to stop doing that?" Abby was confused. "Why? It's trash. Throw it away."

Ben shook his head and sat next to Abby on the ground. "I was throwing the trash to Matt, then he would chuck it into the dumpster." She could hear the sheepishness in his voice. "You told me to stop doing that 'cause one of us could get hurt."

Abby giggled as she remembered the conversation. "Or get smacked in the head. Okay, I remember now." She opened her eyes and smiled at her brother. "I was bending over looking for my keys, thought I dropped them in the trash box by accident . . ."

Matt plopped himself down on the other side of Abby. "Yep. And you stood up right when Fingers Malone there" -- he pointed at Ben and made a face -- "released the old frying pan in my direction."

"Of course. Sounds exactly like me." Abby let out a big breath and smiled at the two. "Tell me we're almost done?"

"Almost. I think Matt and I can handle it from here, right, Matt?" Ben was standing, looking expectantly in Matt's direction.

"Maybe another ten minutes, Abs." Matt smiled at his ex and leaned in slightly, brushing her tangled hair out of her face. "Want some water?"

Suddenly aware of Matt's presence closing in on her, Abby felt a strange tingle course through her body. While she was willing herself to answer him and say yes to some water, she could barely manage to make her head move in the direction of what she thought a nod might look like.

As he got up and walked off, Abby took a second to remind herself of who and what it was she was dealing with here.

He's my ex. He's the one who left me and now I have Andrew and a new life I'm going back to. Her attention was pulled as she watched him straightening his khaki shorts as he stood up from the cooler in the back of his Jeep Cherokee. Yep, that's him, the guy who left me and our plans to get married.

Abby knew that if she wanted to get through this, she needed to remind herself over and over how crappy this man was at one time.

"We're really lucky your head didn't break the frying pan." Ben's face may have been clouded with concern, but he was trying to joke around the fact that he almost killed her.

"I hope I at least put a small dent in it," she chided as she reached up to take the water Matt was offering her. "Thanks."

Matt nodded and returned to his position sitting next to Abby on the ground. "You going to be okay?"

Abby was pressing the unopened water bottle to her temple. "Mm-hmm. I just need a few moments to recover."

"Well, I'm your brother. Half-brother, but we get along okay. Except this morning when I was so hung over I yelled at you for being loud."

"My, my. How quickly the tables turn." The irony of this was not lost on Abby, since just a short time ago when they were forced to live together suddenly, she had dealt with his loudness every morning for weeks. At least until they began to get along. "And, by the way, I'm not waking up out of a coma, I'm just confused."

Ben shrugged. "Figured you could use all the help you can get."

She remembered now calling Matt to arrange him dropping off some of her things. "Okay, I called you," she said, pointing at him, "to drop off my stuff and Ben knew we needed help." She nodded as it all came together. "You're here because we needed some backup."

Matt grinned at his ex-fiancée. "A little nervous you had forgotten something?"

"More like a little nervous I woke up and it was five years ago."

Taking the water bottle out of her hands, he smiled sweetly at her as he opened the cap and handed it back to her, urging her to take a sip. "And would that really be so terrible?"

Abby almost spit her water out. "You tell me, considering you did cheat on me!"

"Okay then!" Ben clapped his hands together and jumped up. "Abby's fine, the truck is almost unloaded. Let's get this done."

Abby smiled at her brother, grateful for the reprieve. "Good plan." She began to stand but felt a little woozy still. "I think I may stay here for another minute if that's okay with you two?"

The boys nodded and Ben headed back to the truck. Matt lingered for an extra moment.

Abby looked up at him as he leaned against the tree, watching her. "Do you need something?"

He shook his head. "I'm sorry."

"I know. I am too." She peered up at him, shielding her eyes from the sun beating down around them, finding its way through the leaves and branches, landing in a scattered fashion on their skin and on the ground around them.

"I can't take it back. But you didn't deserve what I did." He was watching Ben unload, but his words were directed at Abby. As much as she had wanted this kind of apology for so long, she now wanted to just let it go.

"Matt, it's fine. I shouldn't have said that last comment." She followed his line of sight and watched Ben as well. "Honestly, I think I'm happier now, nothing against you or us, but what I ended up with is so much more."

She could feel his body go a little rigid at her words. Abby wanted to make sure he didn't interpret her incorrectly. "Not saying what we had didn't matter. Just that what we had had run its course."

Nodding, he smiled down at her. "You are better than you were before, Abs. I can't put my finger on it, but you've changed."

"Thank you." That was all she needed to hear. "I

needed to change. Now, go over there and help him out while I get my equilibrium back," she said, shooing him away with her hands. "I'm anxious to see the crap of mine you found."

"I'll have to run home and grab it after this. I was in such a hurry to meet you two here, I forgot it." Matt's gaze was thoughtful as he smiled at Abby. "I'm glad you let me help."

Abby watched him as he walked away, realizing that deep in her gut she was feeling a calm she hadn't felt regarding Matt in a long time. It was an emotion that only comes once you truly let go and are able to move forward. It was the moment after sadness and guilt have been exorcised and you can see a former lover for who they truly are.

It was peace.

THE REST OF THE MORNING HAD SNUCK PAST THEM fairly quickly. Ann-Marie had called Matt, and was not pleased when she found out he was with Abby and Ben. Thankfully, he had helped Ben as much as he could before he was called back home.

"I'll call you later. It may have to wait until tomorrow for me to bring your stuff by." He shook Ben's hand and embraced Abby in a one-armed hug before he jumped in his car and took off.

Ben was regarding Abby with a smirk out of the corner

of his eye as they drove the U-Haul down Lankershim Boulevard.

"Quite the heartbreaker, aren't you?"

Abby narrowed her eyes and shot her brother a look. "History lesson: He dumped me."

"That doesn't mean anything, Abby. People change, and even though you weren't good together at one time, or he thought he lost his love for you, you're both different people now. I'm just saying I see the way he looks at you."

"You've got to be kidding me, Ben!" Abby wanted to laugh at the utter ridiculousness of this thought, but her head still hurt too much. "He's got Ann-Marie and I've got Andrew. And anyway, what's done is done."

Ben regarded his sister from his position behind the wheel. "I know you well enough to know that just because something appears to be done doesn't mean it is."

Abby was facing the window, looking out as they passed familiar buildings on their drive. This was home, she thought. It feels so far away now.

"Ben, I've moved on. I've moved on so much that I'm actually moving." She sat up a little taller as she spoke. "I'm physically leaving the state. The last few years have been hard, and I'm ready to move forward."

She turned in her seat to face her brother. "I would sit alone in my living room, and I'd cry, Ben. I had this job I had once loved so, so much and it became the most difficult place to be in the world. My boss was a jerk who used me as a punching bag when things got bad for him, they were losing money and had the threat of closing down hanging over their heads. I had an assistant trying to take my position from me. Then Matt left me." She swallowed back the tears threatening to spill. "To top it off, my mother died. It was all too much."

Abby was looking down at her hands, playing with the rings on her fingers, smiling. "And then things changed."

"Because you were forced to go to St. Kitts?"

"Well, being 'forced' to go to a tropical isle for a little R&R is extreme, but yes, essentially." She smiled at the memory. "Things changed because I was laid off."

She could still see the office, with the CEO and VP sitting there, handing her those papers to sign. The feeling of loss, the sadness at not being wanted, the hurt in her pride as if there was a chink in her armor. Abby had felt all of these things in a wave of emotion that day. Yet, as she sat here reminiscing about that fated moment in time, she felt gratitude.

"Ben, if I hadn't been laid off I wouldn't be here with you. I'm sure eventually we would have met, but I'm glad it's now. You came along in my life when I needed more, and so did Leigh." She took a big breath, feeling the tension in her body release as she added, "We may have lost our mother, but we gained you."

"That's a cool way to look at it, I guess." Ben smiled. "Thanks, Abs."

"Please," she waved her hand in the air, pushing her tears back into their rightful place. "Thank you. And I'm serious when I say I'm grateful. I never thought getting laid off would make me so happy."

"Well, you are just one part of that romantic equation, Abs. The other part, the one named Matt? He still has feelings for you . . . or at least something is going on with that guy."

Abby wasn't sure if she'd heard the sound of a protective brother in his voice, or if it was the sound of a protective best friend for Andrew, but she realized that if Ben thought there was something more, then there very well could be.

"Ben, if you're worried about Andrew, don't be. I would never do anything to hurt him."

He rolled his eyes. "It's not just Andrew I'm worried about, it's you, too."

The air had gotten a little thicker than Abby needed in the main cabin of the U-Haul. As she cracked a window she made sure she appeased Ben's nervous energy.

"You don't need to worry about me at all, Ben. I'm good."

Yet as soon as the words were out of her mouth, Abby had to wonder if she was.

DAY FOUR

"ARE YOU DISCOUNTING ALL OF THE ROOMS?"

Abby wanted to put her head through a plate-glass window. Not out of frustration, but because the remnants of yesterday's injury still lingered.

Still in bed nursing her aching head, Abby was sipping coffee and clearing the fog from all the corners of her mind when she had called Maria to check in. She had received several emails and texts from Maria, who was busy helping to plan a wedding for an ambitious bride-to-be and was up to her ears with lists, itineraries and plans.

La Cantina had agreed to house the wedding party as well as the rehearsal dinner and happy hour on its premises, while the Frigate Beach Hotel was actually hosting the wedding and the majority of guests.

Maria had been running negotiations between the two properties and they aimed to make the wedding weekend as smooth as possible for all parties involved, from shuttling drunk partygoers to arranging cars for the wedding party to and from both hotels. Ziggy had teamed up with Mikey, who was normally a bartender for Ricky's, the bar at the Frigate, and they were taking the wedding guests out on day tours and snorkeling adventures, while Maria and Miss C., also from Ricky's, were organizing trips to the beach and into town for shopping on the Main Street in Basseterre or at Port Zante.

"Yes, Maria, let's go ahead and give them a discount on all of the rooms since we're booked out." Abby knew by discounting the rooms and making sure the bride's parents felt taken care of, she could almost 100% ensure the weekend would be filled with revelry and not rioting. "Also, when they arrive, let's throw in a welcome reception for just the main family members. Insist upon it. Let's do something small and intimate for them around the pool, with rum tasting and traditional fruits and foods. Give them a calm before the storm from us."

Abby could feel Maria's excitement through the phone. "Great idea! You know what . . . my cousin Sherry? Her daughter's best friend is one of the girls over at the nail salon. I'm gonna see if we can get her to do manicures for a reduced rate here on the property."

"Yes! In fact, find a hairdresser, too. Let's see if we can offer services for the bridal party the day of the rehearsal dinner and the wedding day. Aim for a discounted price with them, and let the bride know we will cover her hair and nails for the day. Treat her like a queen."

"Good call. And a very smart one, too." Maria's voice

was full of pride. "You're gonna do this place some good, Abby George!"

Abby's cheeks flushed bright red from the compliment. "I hope so, Maria. Any other news?"

"Well," she began, the tone in her voice making Abby regret even asking, "I did hear a rumor from one of the women in town the other day."

"Do I want to know?" Abby sighed as she made her pillows more comfortable around her neck and shoulders. She could feel tension beginning to gather there and knew she might splurge on a massage before she left California.

"Rhys Industries is planning on taking over as many properties in the Caribbean this year as they can. They bought the plantation on Nevis last week."

Abby sat straight up. "You mean the one Andrew and I went to? With Ben for his break?"

"The very one. Seems they may invest in another there or . . ." Maria's voice had trailed off, either from bad reception or because the news was so brutal Abby wouldn't want to hear it. Since she could hear Maria breathing on the other end of the line, she realized it was the latter.

"Or they are going to try to take La Cantina away from us." Abby felt like the sleepy clouds that had retreated from her head had found their way back in. "Or rather, J.D. wants to take La Cantina away from me. Unbelievable."

Maria was thoughtful as she spoke. "Abby, no one takes anything from you unless you let them, you hear me, girl? Now, finish up there so you get back here. We got a wedding to deal with."

Feeling a remorseful thud deep inside her soul, Abby could only see imminent failure at the moment. She knew in her heart she needed to be positive, but couldn't help feeling she was going to lose this battle.

They're stronger than we are, she thought. They're a corporation, and us . . . ? Her heart was heavy.

"There's nothing that can be done 'bout it now, so stop frettin'. Get your work done there and head back."

"This won't be easy, will it, Maria?" Abby wasn't one to be defeated easily, but realizing she might be up against some serious gunfire on her end had her thinking twice about her decision. Did I make the right one? Can I really pull this off and keep the hotel afloat? Will I end up letting everyone down somehow?

"Were you expecting this to be a walk in the park? You're running a business, girl. So, no, it won't be easy. Nothing's easy." Maria huffed a little into the phone. "If it was, it wouldn't be worth fighting for, now would it?"

Truer words had never been spoken. There was nothing Abby could do now, except close up shop here and then head back to what could be the most difficult fight of her life.

Keeping La Cantina.

Or fending off J.D.?

THE GROCERY STORE BY ABBY'S HOME WAS PACKED. She had chosen to go at five o'clock, right when everyone in L.A. was getting off work and heading home to make dinner and get settled in for the night, or so it seemed. Maneuvering the packed aisle, Abby clung to her little list. Ben had been such a big help to her the last few days that she wanted to do something special for him, so she was making his favorite dish: bangers and mash.

She made her way through the maze of produce, selecting the perfect potatoes and picking up an onion for the recipe. She was headed to the dairy aisle for some milk when she heard a familiar voice. Abby stopped in her tracks, searching her memory bank for the reason it resonated. She held her breath for a minute, listening. No longer able to hear it, she chalked it up to hearing things and pushed on to finish her list.

Next up were the sausages. Making her way over to the meat case, she heard the voice again. This time, she knew who it was, and couldn't wait to see her.

The voice was piping out of the body of a small Asian girl who was standing at the meat case, chatting away on her BlackBerry as she picked through steaks, searching for the perfect one.

"No, Perkins, 'we' can't make it this weekend. I have things to do." The girl pulled the phone away from her ear and made a face at it before thrusting it back to her ear and continuing. "I get it. You want me to attend the meeting with you tomorrow morning, but I can't drop everything. Reschedule either for next weekend or one weeknight next week. Got it?"

Abby stood smiling, watching Elizabeth as she handled the person on the other end of the phone with such grace and ease. Elizabeth had been one of the perks at Abby's last job with CEO Guy. She had single-handedly helped Abby through many moments at work when she thought she couldn't push herself any more than she already had. The two of them had made quite a team together, but in the end Elizabeth's skillset had far outweighed Abby's. Well, at least in the eyes of CEO and VP, so she kept her job when the great layoff happened.

Her call over, Elizabeth all but punched her finger through the phone as she hit End. She plucked the steak of her choice from the bed of meat, tossed it in her basket and whirled around ready for more shopping when she and Abby made eye contact.

"Abby!"

The two girls screamed at the same time and ran to each other, talking at once, hugging and laughing at the same time.

"I left you messages!"

"I know. I left town. I had to, Eliz."

"It was terrible. That place was a pit of darkness. So many people were let go."

"They left me no other choice, I had to get out of L.A. I wasn't sure I could survive looking for a job here."

"We were down to five people in that office. Five. Can you believe it?"

Abby shook her head. The sad thing was she could believe it. "It's so sad, but I'm honestly glad I was let go now." Taking a step back, she surveyed her friend from head to toe. "You look great! How are things over there?"

Elizabeth smiled at her old work buddy. "Oh, girl. I left. Remember the Waters Company?"

Abby couldn't forget the Waters Company. They were such great clients for CEO and his partners, as well as a good group to Abby and Elizabeth. Based in San Francisco, the two gentlemen in charge always insisted Elizabeth and Abby fly in for meetings so they could assist with event planning. Then both girls could be on hand for assisting the executives if needed. Elizabeth was also a marketing whiz and was asked on many occasions to sit in on their discussions, adding her two cents. It was during these trips that Abby learned most of what she now knew about marketing, all from Elizabeth. Calling her a mentor was appropriate, but it didn't seem to give Elizabeth the proper credit. She had helped Abby grow more in their two years together than any class in college or any other job ever would.

"I totally remember them. They had the hot marketing exec who always took us out for drinks." Abby giggled at the memory.

"Todd. Yep, still there." Elizabeth's eyes lit up. "I'm their L.A. liaison now, Abby. They always wanted to open an office here. Chris found the space in Hollywood, off Melrose, and grabbed it for a song. We have four of us operating out of there at the moment, but we're expanding."

Abby's jaw dropped. "You are kidding me? In this economy?"

Elizabeth's grin was contagious. "Yes. Chris and John had a contingency plan in place, and as soon as the shit began hitting the fan for most markets, people closing up shop and whatnot, they went into high gear. Chris had an idea for video streaming he had developed, which the entertainment industry ate up." She shrugged her shoulders. "Not bad to have Paramount and Universal on your roster of new clients in the middle of a recession, huh?"

"Eliz, that is amazing. I'm so happy for you. Well, for all of you. Chris and John have to be ecstatic, they always wanted you working for them. Congratulations!"

"Well, that's why I've been trying to call you forever, Abby. Where the hell have you been?"

Abby smiled at her friend and peered at their grocery baskets. "It's going to take me longer than a minute in a grocery aisle to fill you in." She reached out and grabbed Elizabeth's arm. "Why don't I grab us some wine and snacks and you follow me to my place? I'm making dinner." She held her basket high in the air, dangling it Elizabeth's way like she was showing a puppy a toy it wanted.

"You're cooking? Awesome. I'll grab the wine, you lead the way."

"You're moving to the Caribbean? Are you insane?"

Abby loved that the fact that she had taken over an inn, found her half-brother, fell in love and discovered family secrets had been brushed aside by her old friend. None of that mattered, it was the part about where she was moving that resonated with Elizabeth.

"Not insane, needing a change. Come on. What do I have here?"

Elizabeth was sitting cross-legged on the floor next to Ben. The trio had copped a squat in the middle of the living room, turning over cardboard boxes and using them as makeshift trays for their dinner plates. A dinner Abby had skillfully put together and that had been declared "damn good" by her Brit brother, a compliment she was more than proud to receive.

"Well, you could have a job, for one." Elizabeth tipped her glass in Ben's direction as he filled it with more wine.

"I could have a job?" Abby scoffed at the thought. "Where, Eliz? No one is hiring, and if they were I wouldn't make what I was before."

Elizabeth took a thoughtful sip from her glass. "Are you sure about that?"

"Why? Are you hiring?" Abby's response was as flippant as she felt at the moment.

"Actually, yes. It's what I've been trying to tell you." She took a breath and set her glass down. "Abby, when Chris and John found out you were gone, they were shocked. A lot of us were. You were the glue for that place and one of the only employees who could be thrust into any situation and was malleable. No matter what, you took any chance you were given and ran with it."

Abby felt Ben's eyes watching her, and thought she saw a little pride swimming in them. Embarrassed by Elizabeth's words, she tried to stop her, but Elizabeth pushed on.

"Anyway, the opportunity came for them to open the office here. They called me, made me an offer I couldn't refuse, and the rest is history. They also told me to get the office up and ready to go, and one of the people they have been insisting I add to our crew is you, Abs. Chris and John both ask me at least twice a week if I've found you or heard back from you."

Abby was stunned. "They do?"

"Yes! They love you and really want you in that office with me." Elizabeth shook her head at her friend. "How can you not get that? Of course they want you to be there, ding-dong. And they are prepared to offer you a very competitive salary to start. In fact, they would start you at the same salary you were making when you were let go."

They're nuts. Holy crap. My salary back? Abby's thoughts were in a whirlwind.

"Benefits?" Abby ignored the look of amazement, or maybe it was judgment, aimed her way from Ben's side of the room.

"Yep." Elizabeth bobbed her head up and down. "Benefits, vacation, sick days . . . the works, Abs. You'd still be an executive coordinator, but you'd be in charge of all event planning, PR and media relations." She smiled at her friend knowingly, adding, "We'd hire you an assistant."

"Oh, wow." Abby wanted to have her poker face on but couldn't mask her shock (or maybe it was excitement) at the offer Elizabeth had just made her.

"I know it's a lot to take in, Abs. Especially seeing as you're about to start a whole new life, but" -- Elizabeth leaned across the cardboard boxes and grabbed her friend's hand -- "you have to think about this. I need you to think about this. It's a terrific opportunity, not just for you but for all of us."

"It is a great chance, Abby, but do you need to think about it?" While he sat there so close by, Ben's voice sounded far away. Maybe I'm about to pass out, she thought.

"Of course she does, Ben. Abby had a life here. A home, a job. I can't promise her an island, but I can give her stability at least. A contract and a paycheck coming in." Abby could hear Elizabeth's patient explanation, but knew she was holding back from telling Ben to just shut up.

"But what life? Abby, you said yourself it was hard for you here and you spent a lot of time crying over the last year. Why come back to that?"

Abby opened her mouth to speak, but Elizabeth felt the need to answer for her. "Because this is home, Ben. Matt may have been a shit, but Abby was building her life here. Her life, not one given to her by her sister and not one filled with so much drama, I might add."

"Drama? You think the life she has on St. Kitts is filled with drama? How about having her fiancé leave her for another woman? Or losing her job right before Christmas? Is that not drama?"

Before Elizabeth could answer or Ben could raise his voice any louder, Abby held up both of her hands at the pair. "Please, you two. Stop. For me?"

The duo exchanged a look, turning their attention back to Abby, who sat with her hands folded in her lap.

"Ben, you're right. I had no life here for the last year. I know that." She looked around her living room, once filled with her mish-mosh items and vintage finds, now sitting eerily empty. "We've packed up this place and part of me is more than ready to move forward. Then I run into you." She smiled at her old friend. "And yes, this chance is one that I would be crazy to not think about, no matter what my plans for the future are at the moment. I'm blown away at the package you're presenting me and I need a little time to think about this."

Ignoring the daggered look from her brother, Abby continued. "Look, I'm set to fly out in a few days. Matt is dropping off some stuff for me tonight that I need to pack, or maybe now unpack, whatever the case may be. Either way I'm going to take at least 24 hours to sit on this and make a decision."

Ben started to interrupt, but Abby thwarted him before he could begin. "I know the implications of this,

Ben, if I say yes and stay in L.A. But right now, I want to weigh my options. All of them. Okay? And if you think I'm being selfish or you don't agree with me, then I'm sorry."

Elizabeth stood up and held out her hands to Abby, helping her friend up off the floor. "Good. Well, I'm glad you're at least going to think about it." She looked at her watch. "It's almost eight and I need to get home. Call me if you have any questions, okay?"

Abby enveloped her friend in a big hug. "You got it. Either way you'll hear from me tomorrow night."

Even in his irritation, Ben minded his manners and stood to say good-bye to Elizabeth. "It was nice meeting you, you evil temptress."

"Ha. I've been called worse." She smiled and embraced Ben as well. "I'm so glad to meet you, and I'm sorry if this causes any issue here. I had to let her know she was wanted." Elizabeth looked Ben square in the eyes. "Wouldn't you want to know if someone wanted you?"

They said their good-byes as Abby walked her to the door. When she returned, Ben was already filling up their glasses, his jaw tight and his body language reflecting his upset with crossed arms and hunched shoulders.

Bracing herself, Abby took her glass and waited for Ben to attack. But he didn't.

"I can't promise to understand why you need time to think about it, but I want you to take whatever time you need. For once I'm going to shut up and let you just figure it out."

Abby lowered herself back to the floor, landing next to her brother with their knees touching. "Thanks. I needed to hear just that." She shook her head and stared into her wineglass. "I cannot believe that offer, can you?"

"Hell no. It's a good one." He slugged her in her forearm playfully. "And you've had a lot change. We both have." Ben stared off into space. "I wanted you to know I'm thinking about deferring a year when the semester is over so I can spend a little more time on the island with you," he whispered.

Let the surprises continue. "What? Ben, you can't do that. You cannot stop your schooling this close to the end."

"I'm thinking about it. I haven't made up my mind, but I'm thinking about it." He shrugged his shoulders. "It's an option, and as you like to say, it's important to have options."

Admiring her brother's wisdom, she shoulder-butted him and took a sip from her glass. "Yeah. Options."

It was at that moment her phone signaled an incoming text. Much to her surprise, she didn't have just one, but several appeared. The first few were Andrew saying hello and sending her pictures from London, the view from his flat in Richmond overlooking the park and one of him having a pint at his local pub. Thank God for modern technology, Abby thought as she smiled and looked at his pictures, missing him a little more than she had when she'd woken up that morning.

Another one was from J.D. He had taken a picture

from his room at the hotel of the sun setting over the water. It was a gorgeous sight to behold and one he knew would elicit an emotional response from her. She left that text chain to see who the other one was from, vowing to deal with him later.

The last one was from Matt, saying he couldn't make it tonight but would stop by tomorrow with the box. Ann-Marie was still mad at him and he had to wait until she went to work before he came by. She shook her head, amused by it all. She quickly sent replies to Andrew and Matt, promising Andrew to video-chat in a few hours and telling Matt tomorrow was fine, and ignored J.D. altogether.

When she pried herself away from her iPhone, Abby's tired eyes met Ben's teasing stare.

"More options, Abs?"

Busted, her cheeks flushed a bright red. "You could say that."

DAY FIVE

"You look tired, Abs."

Abby smiled at her computer, too happy to see Andrew's face staring back at her to care how tired she looked or even felt at the moment.

"I know. I am tired. We had a lot to get done here, plus getting Ben out to see some of the sights. It's been a whirlwind trip."

Andrew tilted his head to the side, smiling at her over the airwaves. "I hope you're taking time for yourself?"

"Ha!" was the only response she could muster. She turned on her side to adjust her laptop so she could see him a bit better. Abby was sprawled out on her bed, drinking her coffee and greeting the day as Andrew was winding his down at the office in London.

"You know, I'll be back on St. Kitts in about two or three weeks. We start the initial planning phase at that time and we're all meeting there to get the ball rolling."

Abby felt her tummy turn over once. The offer from Elizabeth was still weighing heavily on her and she had yet to bring it up to Andrew. She wasn't sure if she would make herself feel better or worse by telling him. It's like when you cheat on someone and tell them about it to ease your own guilt, she mused.

"That's good news. For me." Abby smiled coyly. She wanted to tell him about the offer but felt that the air around her was saturated by the silence she still needed while she made up her mind. It was an internal struggle for Abby, as she believed in honesty with those around her, especially with someone she was building a relationship with. No matter what the distance.

Andrew must have seen her hesitation, because he didn't let her distracted answers roll idly by. "Abs, where are you today? I know you've got a lot going on, but you seem like you've checked out. You okay?"

Abby sat up and leaned against the headrest of the bed, propping the computer in her lap. She opened her mouth and closed it again quickly, stopping the words from escaping. Andrew watched her, and had even stopped shuffling papers so he could sit down at his desk and give her his full attention.

"I was offered a job here. It's a good one, with benefits and room for growth. Plus they'd start me at my old salary."

Abby watched Andrew's face for his reaction. He nodded, averting his eyes from the screen, and pursed his lips together in quiet contemplation. "Okay. And what are you thinking?"

Abby shrugged her shoulders. "That's just it. I don't know what I'm thinking, Andrew. About any of this. I'm packing up my life and moving to an island. An island! It's great and crazy, but am I being too crazy?"

"Well, only one person can answer that Abby, and it's you." He turned back to the screen and looked directly into the camera, speaking to Abby. "Your sister will be more than disappointed, you know."

And that's the one thing I don't need to hear right now, she thought.

"I'm quite aware of what this could mean, Andrew. I'm not saying I'll be taking it; I just need to weigh it out right now. It's an option, and a few months ago I didn't have any. Now I have several. I'm walking away from a life here and it's a big deal, do you see that?"

"Abby, you told me yourself it wasn't much of a life. Why would you question a decision you already made?" Andrew's words surprised Abby, but she made a choice to ignore them for the moment and let him say his piece. "You decided to stay on the island. You fought your sister for the chance and promised people, like Maria and Ziggy, you would do wonderful things. Now you are questioning this? How?"

"I'm not questioning anything, I'm just looking at all of my . . ." Abby didn't get to finish her sentence.

"Options. I know, you're making it abundantly clear you like having them."

Abby felt as if she had been slapped across the face by his words. "Why are you irritated with me? I've not made a fast and sure decision and I feel like you're persecuting me for no reason."

"I'm not persecuting you, I'm just telling you how it is, Abby. You're being selfish but you can't see it." His head shook in disappointment. "You do realize your actions have consequences, don't you?"

Wow. Abby knew this had gone too far now. Shaking her head, stunned at his reaction, she sat up, preparing to sign off.

"I'm going to go, it's the best thing to do right now. I don't think this conversation could end well, so can we please talk later?"

Andrew abruptly stood up in front of the computer, shoving papers in his computer bag and making a show of gathering his things in the office. "Not sure where I'll be later. I have a few options here for dinner plans tonight. I like keeping them free, you know. My options."

"Andrew, stop it. Stop using that word. . . ."

Andrew smiled tight and sweet at his computer screen. "What word? 'Options'? Why, Abs? Isn't life about having them?"

That was it. "You know what, Andrew, this is why I hesitated at us being together. The distance? No. I figured with modern-freakin'-technology we'd be fine. Your age? No, I mean it was a bit of a hurdle, but not an issue. But, hey, guess what? Your friend Ben? He's being beyond supportive right now of me and whatever choice I make.

He gets it, Andrew, that I need to weigh my . . . yep, gonna say it again . . . options!" She took a breath, making sure she had his attention, and continued her rant. "No, I hesitated because relationships take work. Lots of work, and sometimes they may not be fun, but no matter what, two people who may or may not be falling for each other, they show up for each other." She shook her head at the screen, fighting the tears threatening to escape. "They show up and are supportive and loving. I got a great offer, and you may very well get one yourself one day, changing your course of action or the life path you're on. You don't know. We never know when our lives could change. So don't judge me, Andrew, and don't tell me who or what my thinking about things may just be affecting, because guess what? I already know."

Abby's hand had absentmindedly found its way to her cheek, brushing away the tears that had begun to spill. Glancing at the computer screen, she saw that Andrew's jaw was set, but he was still listening.

But she had nothing else to say.

The pair sat in silence for a few minutes before a tap at Abby's bedroom door interrupted them. It was Ben and he had her phone in his hand.

"Hey, Matt's on the phone for you." He walked in to hand the phone to her, not realizing that she was on the computer with Andrew. "He wants to decide on a time to come by."

Ben noticed Abby's sullen look and tears a bit too late. He peered at her computer and saw Andrew's glare on the screen. Ben began backing out of the room, pointing to the phone and shrugging his shoulders, silently miming "What should I do?"

"Just tell him I'll call him back when I'm free." Abby watched him leave, mouthing "I'm sorry" to her the whole way. Once the door closed, she brought her attention back to Andrew, who was primed and shaking his head.

"Matt?"

Seriously?

"Yes, Matt. He's coming by with some of my things he found after he moved out."

"So you get a job offer and now you're seeing your ex?"

Abby held up her hand to stop him before he went way overboard to an area of jealousy she knew she couldn't handle right now.

"I'm ending this here for now. I'm not sure what you think is happening and I can only tell you to stop thinking it. I have to go."

This time, the two locked eyes and stared at each other through their screens, Abby wishing she could alleviate any fears of his, but not sure how when she couldn't even alleviate her own. And this whole other side of him was another topic to discuss down the road. She wasn't sure what she thought of this Andrew and needed time to sort her thoughts out.

"Okay." Andrew nodded, breaking the silence. "We'll talk later?"

Not able to say yes or no, Abby just nodded. "Have a good dinner. 'Bye, Andrew."

And she disconnected the call.

THE DAY SLID BY UNEVENTFULLY FOR ABBY AFTER HER argument with Andrew. Still unsure of her plans, she kept packing her things and prepping for their flight out the next day. Ben needed to get out for a bit and wanted to see the Walk of Fame in Hollywood, so they made an afternoon of it.

They walked to the metro, taking the red line from North Hollywood to Hollywood and Highland. Abby dragged Ben up and down Hollywood Boulevard looking at the names, into the Wax Museum, and they had matched their hand- and footprints with the ones memorialized in front of Grauman's Chinese Theatre. She took him to a nearby diner on Hollywood Boulevard for lunch and bought him a fake Oscar with the title "Best Brother Award" for him to take back. She was moving at a fast clip the whole afternoon, not to pack in all the sights, but because she just couldn't bear the thought of thinking anymore.

As they were taking pictures in front of the Capitol Records Building, Abby's phone started ringing. Hoping it was Andrew so they could make things right, she grabbed for it and answered without looking to see who it was.

"Hello?" Her salutation was overly excited and filled with anticipation.

"That's more than enthusiastic. It's Matt."

Abby's heart went thud into her stomach as it washed over her that it wasn't Andrew. "Hey. Sorry I haven't called you. It's been hectic today."

"No problem. Just wanted to come by tonight to drop off your things, cool?"

"Um, yeah. That's great, Matt. Seven o'clock work for you?"

"Yep. Ann-Marie will be out with her friends tonight so I won't catch hell." He chuckled into the phone. "It's really stupid, huh?"

"Yes, Matt, it's stupid she would be upset you're meeting your ex. Of course the fact the two of you got together while we were still engaged seems to have escaped your memory bank. So I'm sure she's just worried that you may try to pull a fast one. Or maybe she thinks I will. Don't know, Matt." Abby was really annoyed, not even with Matt, but at the situation all around.

"And that's the girl I know and love." Matt was surprised, but took it with ease. "Guess I kind of deserved that. I thought we were past it, but I get it."

You would take that in stride, wouldn't you? She thought. One of the traits she had loved about Matt was how laid back he was and opposed to drama. He was great at taking things as they came. He never liked to get ahead of himself nor did he like to look back.

"Sorry," Abby sighed into her cell. She was watching

ANNE KEMP

Ben take pictures of himself making it look like the cylindrical Capitol Records Building was coming out of his head. "It's been a rough morning. We are past it, it's just other people around me aren't."

"Insert knowing nod from ex here."

"Huh?"

"If I were there, I'd empathize with you. I'm sure your boyfriend now isn't pleased to know we reconnected."

"I didn't even have time to tell him the whole story. It's complicated, Matt. You know how that goes, right?"

Matt chuckled on the other end. "Do I. We can talk about it later if you want, but right now let's say seven, all right?"

"Perfect. See ya then."

She disconnected the call and placed her phone back in her bag. Looking around for Ben, she realized he was making his way down the hill on Vine and heading to the corner of Hollywood Boulevard again. She scampered to catch up to him, linking her arm in his and laying her head on his shoulder. She warmed instantly, feeling safe and steady. She was grateful she had this time with her baby brother and she was thankful he was here while she was navigating this part of her life.

"So, do you want to go see anything else? Maybe go check out Gower Gulch down the street? It's where the actors who wanted to play cowboys would gather back in the day, waiting for work on set."

Ben shook his head. "Nah, I was thinking we should

70

get back, Abby. You've spent the day avoiding your decision. Why don't we go home so you can make one?"

Abby nodded in agreement. "You are so right on."

Abby felt him pull his arm away from where they were linked at the elbows and stopped her so they could face off on the street.

"Whatever you decide, I support it, okay? Even if it pisses anyone off."

She nodded and smiled at her brother. "Come on, we'll grab some takeout on the walk back from the metro, cool?"

"Cool. As long as I get to pick the spot."

"I wouldn't have it any other way, trust me." She looked ahead and saw the entrance to the metro just ahead. "In fact, I'll pay for it if you can beat me to the train station!"

Abby then took off a few steps ahead of Ben before he realized what the game was. She heard him racing up behind her, and let him take the lead, as she never intended to have him pay for their food anyway.

She just liked that she had someone here to play with.

"This place is empty!"

Matt was in shock when he entered the old apartment he and Abby had shared. It was spotless, the living room only housing their suitcases, a couch and a small cot Abby had borrowed from one of her neighbors for the night. All the leftover furniture was either being picked up by Goodwill in the morning or had been claimed by neighbors in the building.

Abby was gripping the box Matt had handed her tightly. She made her way over to their makeshift cardboard coffee table and flounced herself onto the floor so she could dig inside.

"Wine?"

She looked up to see Matt dangling a nice bottle of red in front of her and holding plastic cups. The moment rang of familiarity as she was taken back to the time when they had moved in, years ago.

"Remember the night we moved in here?" He was in the same memory thread as she.

"Just thinking about it, actually. A couch, no table, no bed yet. I don't think we even had electricity the first night, did we?"

Matt laughed at the thought. "No, we lit candles and sat up talking all night." He seemed sad at the thought. "We had fun, huh?"

Abby grinned up at him from her spot on the floor. "We did."

Matt leaned in close to Abby, inspecting her temple. "How's the head?"

She turned her face to meet his, which put her lips within a few inches of his. She felt his breath on her cheek as he leaned in closer, looking at where her head had been smacked the day before.

"Sore, but I'll be fine." Her eyes met his, and for a

moment she felt something click inside of her while she looked in his eyes. It was all too reminiscent of what they'd had before; his proximity was tempting and her guard was down. There was a pull happening. Matt's eyes trailed down to her lips and he was moving in a little closer.

They were interrupted by a commotion in the hallway as Ben bounded into the room. "Hey, mate! Didn't hear you come in."

Pulling apart before Ben entered the room, Abby watched as he and Matt shook hands. Ben nodded at the bottle in Matt's hand but kept his eyes on Abby. "Is that to celebrate the staying or going?"

Abby rolled her eyes. "I didn't tell him about the possibly staying part, so it's not for that. He may be celebrating that we're leaving." Abby looked at Matt. "Are you?"

Matt didn't answer; instead he held the bottle aloft and asked, "Wine opener?"

"Good man. Never answer a loaded question. Here, follow me and we can get that open." Ben led Matt into the kitchen as Abby began going through the box, shaking off the moment before.

There weren't a lot of items in the old worn-out box. Matt had done his best to keep it safe, but it had suffered some wear and tear while being shuffled from garage to storage unit and back again. Apparently he had moved it several times over the last year or so, always intending to get it back to her but never finding the time.

Abby began by pulling out her old college T-shirt that was wrapped loosely around some old photos of her and Matt. Just finding these made her smile; they were really good pictures. She had saved them not for walks down memory lane, but because the frames were stunning. After Matt left she would take the photos out and pack the frames properly. Beyond the frames, wrinkled and shoved to the side, was a pile of papers. Upon further inspection Abby realized it was the lease from the very apartment she sat in presently. On the opposite side of the box, tucked around an old shoebox, were a few candles. Not just any candles, but Abby's favorite ones made by Voluspa and Votivo. She pulled them out, placing them next to her to pack as well, reaching for the shoebox. Not sure what could be stored in there, she peeled off the tattered lid and found more treasures hidden inside.

Inside the shoebox were a few old scarves Abby recognized as her mother's and some birthday cards from her mom and Leigh she had saved over the years. Hidden beneath the scarves was a small jewelry box tied shut with colorful ribbons.

I don't remember this, she thought as she pulled it out for further inspection.

From the kitchen, she could hear Matt and Ben rattling on, discussing the difference between rugby and American football. Ironic, she thought. Those two would have gotten along very well and been extremely close if Matt and I had stayed together. Would I have ever met Ben if Matt and I had stayed together?

Shaking off the thought, Abby pulled on the delicate ribbon, letting it fall away so she could open the small box. Inside the box, settled on a cloud of fluffy, yellowed cotton, was a tiny anchor charm with a heart decoration. Looking closer, Abby spotted a sapphire set in the heart, sparkling in the light, its twinkling facets lighting up the tiny box where it lay. As she reached in to pull it out, her own bracelet jangled, making her smile as she thought of Andrew. It had been his gift to her, and now they were arguing. Ahhh, love.

Abby stood and walked over to the lit sconce on the wall and stood there inspecting the charm. She was so engrossed in the detail she didn't notice that Ben and Matt had walked back into the room.

"Find anything good?" Matt's voice startled her back to the present moment.

"This." Abby held up the charm for the boys to see. "It's a charm for a necklace, I think."

"Or for a bracelet, Abs." Ben nodded his head in her direction, eyeing her jewelry as it dangled delicately on her wrist. "Like the one you're wearing."

"I didn't even think about that. I'll have to get this added to it." She smiled, elated at the idea. "I think it was my mom's, but I'm not sure. It doesn't look like it was ever used, more like it was wrapped up and put away for safekeeping."

Matt stepped closer to her so he could see as well. "You don't remember it?"

Abby shook her head and looked up, acutely aware of

his presence at the moment. "No, but then again I don't know most of the inventory of my own closet."

In the bottom of the jewelry box lay a slip of paper. Abby took it out, reading it out loud. "'D.S. 15.' Wonder what that is?"

"I never went through the box at all, just saw its contents and knew it was yours." Matt shrugged. "Sorry, I can't help with where it came from."

Abby stared at the anchor for a minute longer. Deep in her gut, she felt she had seen it before, but wasn't at all sure. She looked at the paper again, wondering if the "D.S. 15" was a reminder or a clue as to where it came from. She held it in her hand, turning it over, looking for something to jog her memory. As she went to place the charm back in the box, she noticed some tiny scratch marks on the anchor. Squinting her eyes, she held it closer, trying to make out if the scratches were evidence of wear and tear through the years or maybe something engraved on it. Unsure since she couldn't really see what it was, she placed the small charm back in its box. She set it to the side so she could pack it with her things for safekeeping and placed the shoebox off to the side as well.

Reaching inside the bigger box, she pulled out a few more old T-shirts and some books. Grabbing the hardcovers from their resting place, she hauled them out into her lap for further inspection. One was her first Nancy Drew novel, The Secret of the Old Clock. It was still in pristine condition, as Leigh had her take great care of it when she was little. It had always been one of her favorites. There was another book, one that her mother had given her father for his birthday one year. It was a photography book with photos from the Associated Press compiled from over the years, called Moments in TIME. Seeing this book made Abby's heart sigh just a little, as she could still remember the birthday dinner when the gift was given.

There was a third book, and this one brought a big smile to Abby's face. Clutching her old copy of Treasure Island, she could still remember the summer trip they were on when her father had given it to her. They were staying at their condo on Ocracoke Island, on the Outer Banks in North Carolina. The family vacationed there every summer, her mother and sister basking in the sun on the beach and her father taking their sailboat out as often as he could. He usually had Abby in tow when he would go out on the boat at six a.m. for coffee and a jaunt in the Atlantic. It was their special time together, when they would talk about anything from how the Orioles were doing (because they both loved baseball) to what boys annoyed Abby at school. Her father would sometimes hide books on the boat so she had to find them, setting up a treasure hunt for her. She sighed at the memory.

The day would begin with Abby waking to find a piece of paper, usually placed on the pillow next to her. She would sit up in bed, excited and knowing it was her own private treasure map. She'd greedily dive into it, taking in the drawing her father had penciled for her. In the past, he had set up hunts around the condo, on the boat or in the community itself, even getting the neighbors in on the game. It usually ended with Abby finding a treasure buried somewhere close-by, and the treasures had ranged from books to play jewelry to toys. One time he'd even buried a kite. She'd loved this game.

It was during one of these treasure hunts that Abby had found the book. Her map that morning had led her straight to the sailboat, where her dad was waiting for her on deck. As she'd scampered on board, he had met her, greeting her with a small plastic bag.

"Treasure Island?"

"Yep." Stanley took the book from her hands and thumbed through the pages. "It's a great, complex story. There's mutiny, battles at sea and some treasure hunting. I'm sure it will keep you busy."

"I love treasure!" Abby took the book back from her father's grasp, giggling. "Wait. Why didn't you bury this one this time?"

"Well," Stanley replied as he sat next to his baby girl and pulled her into his one-armed embrace, "I know how much you love treasure. And this book in particular is very special, Abby. I'll need you to protect it for me, okay?"

Abby was so busy flipping through the pages, she barely noticed her father wiping away a tear escaping own his cheek.

"Daddy?" Abby closed the book, staring intently at her father. "Why are you upset?"

Stanley smiled at his daughter. "Because you are growing up so fast. This might just be the last summer I can get you to play this game with me." He sat back to take her in, brushing a piece of hair out of her eyes. "You'll be 16 years old next time we're here. I may not be enough for you. These treasure hunts may not be enough for you."

"Are you kidding?" Abby was appalled at the notion. "I love the maps and the hunt. It's the puzzle of finding where you put things or figuring out from your clues where to go next that makes it so much fun."

They were sitting on the deck, the waves lapping languidly against the hull of the boat. Abby knew in her heart he was right, but she also knew she would always be his girl. She liked being Daddy's Girl. She had snuggled in closer to her father, hugging her book close. "Don't stop sending me on treasure hunts, okay? I love them, Daddy."

Stanley smiled and held her close. "I know you do."

It was their last summer together.

Abby held the book close to her chest, much as she had the day it was given to her, as she sat on the floor of her small apartment. So many decisions in so little time, she thought. I'm so tired of making decisions.

She sat in silent meditation, opening the books and flipping through them, gazing at the pictures in the TIME photo journal, and grinning as she skimmed through Nancy Drew. Funny how books can bring memories rushing to the surface, ones long ago buried, she thought. Each time she touched Treasure Island, a feeling of loss and remembrance coursed through her. She began flipping through the pages, giggling at the notes she had made and sentences she had highlighted.

As she was about to close the book, it turned at such an angle in which it managed to pivot right out of her hand and landed in a thud on the floor in front of her. As it hit the hardwood, a folded sheet of paper floated through the air and landed just outside of Abby's reach.

Great, I probably just ripped a page out of this book. Abby sighed. She stretched out, securing it with her fingertips and sliding the paper closer to her for inspection. It was yellowed, so she knew it was old and worn down. It was folded in half, but she could make out handwriting on the inside. Curious, she opened the paper to see what was written.

Scribbled on the middle of the page at a slight angle in her father's handwriting were numbers: 17.00 and 63.04. But it was the other reference noted at the bottom of the page that made Abby take pause.

D.S. 15?

She cocked her head to one side, wondering what this was. There was nothing else written anywhere on the page. She turned the paper over to the other side, making sure. Nothing. She opened the jewelry box, removing the anchor charm from its home, and toyed with it again, double-checking the note included with this find. D.S. 15.

She sat holding the book and the anchor, looking at the papers, wondering if they were somehow related. Or maybe my imagination is looking for something, she thought. Maybe I just need something to hold on to right now with everything in such a state of flux around me.

Unsure what to do with her finds, she opted to fold up

the larger sheet of paper, placing it back into the book and tucking it to the side with the jewelry box. She started to say something to the guys, but they were chatting away about Ben's schooling and how it felt finding out he had a family he hadn't known about. Not wanting to interrupt, she closed her eyes and felt the hardcover of the book against the palms of her hands, stroking it slowly with the tips of her fingers, taking comfort in having another piece of her father back with her. She would wait until she was alone to study the items, and figure out if there was something to them.

The anchor could be Mom's, or meant for her, she deduced. Then another possibility came to mind. Or Carla. It could have been a gift for Carla Stenson.

Known to Abby and her sister as Carla, the woman who was their father's mistress, Carla was known to Ben as Mom.

Shaking off the thought, Abby sought solace in the fact that she had Treasure Island again and could add it to the plethora of items she was taking with her back to St. Kitts.

If I don't end up staying here, that is.

Opening her eyes, Abby looked around the room at all of the boxes, fighting an overwhelming desire to jump up and kick them. Knowing that would solve nothing, she turned her attention inward as she sorted through her thoughts.

"You okay?" Matt asked.

Abby nodded. "Just overwhelmed."

"Job thoughts?" Ben interrupted.

Abby nodded. "Yes." She glanced at him, sitting next to Matt on the couch. Both of them watching her with steady gazes, not knowing if they should talk or leave her alone.

"Why job thoughts? You own an inn."

"I do indeed, Matt." Abby stood up, taking the books and the other items he had brought her, and began packing them in one of her suitcases. "However, that stinking Elizabeth stopped by and offered me a good job. Here."

She couldn't be sure, but Abby thought Matt's eyes might have lit up ever so slightly.

"Really? So you'd stay?"

Nodding, she continued packing. Each move was deliberate, as if she was weighing her decision by how fluid her own movements were. "I would. If I say yes."

"If? Are you thinking your answer may be yes?" Ben shifted in his seat so he could lean forward, listening more intently to his sister.

She smiled at Ben, and waved Treasure Island in the air. "Not sure, but I think my dad gave me a sign today."

He sighed and hung his head. "You're killing me with this making-up-your-mind business. Our flight leaves tomorrow at 11 a.m.. How long are you going to take?"

Matt shook his head, and patted Ben's knee. "Dude, she likes her options."

Abby giggled as Ben rolled his eyes. "We were together for like five years, Ben. He knows me."

Ben stood up, threw his wine back and disappeared into the kitchen. Abby was still laughing when she and Matt locked eyes. He was smiling at her, watching her move as she drank her wine and packed.

"You seem like you've made up your mind to me, Abs," he said. His voice was soft and hushed. "You're still packing."

"I want to be prepared either way." She shrugged as she picked the bottle up from the floor and refilled her glass. "No matter what, I have to leave the apartment. I gave it up. It's all kind of up to me right now."

She could feel Matt's eyes caressing her body as he took her in from the top of her head to the tips of her toes. "I can think of a few good reasons for you to stay."

Abby felt her body shudder. "Mm-hmm. Is one of them named Ann-Marie?" She turned to meet his stare straight on. "Seriously. Is it?"

He sighed and stood up, crossing the room to stand in front of her.

"Abby." He stopped and put his hands on her arms, looking into her eyes as if he was testing the waters.

Abby felt the familiar pull she'd had with Matt kicking in and knew it was dangerous being this close, no matter what the situation. Still reeling from her argument with Andrew, and standing in the home she used to share with this man, she felt a little more vulnerable than was the norm.

Luckily, Ben came charging in the room, stopping the

moment in its tracks. Abby said a silent thank-you to the gods for watching out for her.

"I'm starving. You two hungry?"

Abby clapped her hands together, delighted. "Yep! I'm starving. What are you thinking? Should we go out?"

"Nah." Ben was shaking his head. "I want to take a few pictures and call Tracey. You guys wait here, it's cool. I'll grab something to go for us."

You are so oblivious! Abby screamed internally. She half-expected Matt to insist they go with him, but was shocked when he reached for his wallet and grabbed some cash, thrusting it in Ben's direction.

"Here you go, my treat. Not sure if you two are staying in L.A. or going, but either way, I want to buy."

"Well, aren't you just downright charitable?" Abby knew he was making a play for them to be alone. The part that scared her was that she wanted to be alone with him, too. It was a thought that both thrilled her and made her slightly nauseated at the same time.

"Contrary to popular belief, I can be quite a decent fellow, Miss George."

Abby put a hand on her hip and cocked her head to the side. "Is that so?"

Ben was completely unaware of the game unfolding in front of him. "So, pizza? Chinese?"

"Pizza." Abby and Matt answered in unison.

"Great. I'll grab a large cheese and a pepperoni. Let me know if you want anything else." He waved at them and headed out the door.

Abby had to give Matt credit. He waited until he heard the door shut before he moved over to the side of the room where she had retreated.

"So, Abby, if you were to stay," he began. She just wasn't sure if she should let him finish.

"Matt, I don't know what I'm doing." She was trying to keep eye contact with him, but was walking backward in a failed attempt to get away from him at the same time. In the process, she was cornering herself with no outlet to speak of for escape.

"Abs, there have been times in my life I haven't known what the hell I was doing either." His voice was low, husky and silky as he kept moving slowly toward her. Abby could feel her heart racing faster. The palpitations were setting off an earthquake of epic proportions inside her chest.

"I get it, Matt, and look. We've moved on, okay?" Her voice was much softer now as well, her whisper laced with a slight tremor from her nerves. Or was it excitement?

Her back hit the wall as the realization hit her that she was literally backed into a corner. Surrounded by boxes, memories and her ex, Abby had no place to go.

Matt pressed his body against hers, using the tips of his fingers to trace their way up her arms to the base of her neck. "I can't stop thinking about you, Abs."

She closed her eyes and tried not to enjoy the feeling of his skin tracing outlines on hers. She leaned her head back into the corner, opening her eyes, attempting to take back the moment. "We can't do this, Matt."

He smiled at her, his charm oozing, sporting a grin

like the cat that had caught the canary. "It's nothing we haven't done before."

"I'm being serious." She looked at him, pleading with her eyes. "We can't."

Matt thrust his hips into hers, making it more than obvious what it was he wanted at the moment. Abby felt her stomach seize as she tilted her head back. She craned her neck to look at him, and using all of her will she pushed herself off the wall against his body in an attempt to move him back enough for her to move away. Unfortunately, her plan failed, and miserably.

Mistaking the push of her body as a "yes" to his advances, Matt grabbed Abby around her waist and fully pulled her into him, covering her mouth with his, kissing her with more passion than he ever had when they'd been together. Abby knew her mission was to stop it, but for some reason the taste of his mouth and feel of his lips made it a lost cause. She struggled for only a second before melting back into his arms, reaching her hands up into his hair and tugging it as she pulled his mouth harder onto hers. She felt elated, guilty, excited, aroused and shockingly in control.

Matt picked her up and was angling to get her on the couch, but she wrapped her legs around his waist, a good move on her part from the groan coming from deep within his body. Stumbling, he walked toward the kitchen, vying for countertop and steady ground. Abby made his walk as difficult as she could, teasing him with soft kisses that hit their mark, trailing up his neck to his earlobes.

They reached the counter, Matt haphazardly dropping her to its sleek, freshly cleaned tile surface in his haste to get her where he thought he could have his way with her. He pulled away, smiling at her, kissing her forehead, and whispered, "I've missed you," as he brought his left hand up the front of her shirt, caressing her breast on the outside of her bra.

She knew she had to snap out of it, to come to her senses. Abby pulled away from Matt, but his arm was wrapped tightly around her waist, pulling her forward, forcing her hips to tilt at an angle into his that was all too familiar and comfortable. Even as she pulled back from his lips, she felt the heat between them grow hotter, and found she was gripping his shirtsleeves as she pulled him harder into her body.

In the back of her head she felt empowered, as if she was cashing in on something she was owed. Hadn't Ann-Marie done this very same deed with Matt when Abby was out of town? Had he not done these things behind her back with someone else? Why shouldn't she be able to do this, too?

Matt's hands had found their way into her hair, pulling it ever so lightly, his fingers becoming tangled in her tresses. It was forcing her head back at an angle that allowed him easier access to the part of her neck that he knew made her more vulnerable. Abby's eyes were closed and she felt his lips brushing against their prey, nibbling and biting her in a seductive dance. She couldn't stop the small moan escaping her lips, which was not only fortunate but also most unfortunate, as it brought her back to present and reminded her of something very important. It was something more important than revenge or a faux feeling of empowerment.

Andrew.

Abby pushed Matt away. He tripped backward, thrown slightly off-balance, then grinned and made his way back to her as if they were playing a game. As he leaned in to grab her off the counter, Abby held both hands out and shook her head.

"No."

Matt combed his hair with his fingers, his face perplexed and flushed. "What? No?"

Abby nodded. "I can't do this. To Andrew, to Ann-Marie. Hell, I can't do it to me. No more. That was a cute walk down memory lane, but not one I should have taken."

Matt shook his head in disbelief. "I don't believe it." He leaned on the counter opposite Abby. "Really?"

It was Abby's turn to return the look of disbelief. "Yes, Matt, really. I won't hurt Andrew like this. It's stupid." She sighed, closing her eyes, and leaned her body against the cabinets behind her. "I already feel guilty enough it got to this point. I'm not this girl and it wasn't right." Abby looked up, expecting to see Matt with his aloof face, but found him wearing a look of total confusion. "I just can't."

She waited for him to be mad or say something absolutely unwelcome, and was surprised when he was quiet.

He must be feeling really bad now, too. God, we are so stupid! Her thoughts were nonstop, beating her up inside and out.

Abby waited a second to get her composure before she jumped off the counter. She smoothed her shirt and took the time to straighten her hair, all the while keeping her eyes trained on Matt. He was refusing to look at her and it made her feel even more terrible. Which is beyond ironic, she thought sarcastically.

"I really did miss you, Abby." Matt's words were slow and thoughtful.

He had still not met her gaze, but she leaned against the counter anyway, waiting. Matt was smiling, granted it was at the floor, but he continued on.

"I'm not happy, and seeing you made me realize where I messed up." He slowly raised his head so their eyes met. "This kind of made it official for me that you'll be 'the one that got away.'"

Abby meet his stare with a bittersweet smile. If ever asked for a description of how she felt in this moment, she would answer that it tasted of sadness and water not quite under the bridge. And guilt. Jesus, she felt guilt.

And it hurt.

"I think," she began, knowing for once exactly what needed to be said and knowing exactly what she needed to do, "you should go."

The mood of the room had shifted so intensely and so fast, it was as if a cold front had moved in over an 80-

degree afternoon. Matt stood up straight, nodding. "I messed up."

Abby shook her head. "I think this time, we both did."

"But if I hadn't messed up the first time, we wouldn't be in this place right now. We'd be . . ."

Abby knew where he was going with this and threw her hand up to stop him. "Just, please, go." No matter what, she couldn't, didn't and wasn't going to hear him utter the words that they could have been married by now.

Instead, she walked to the front hallway and opened the door for him. He stood there, looking beaten and sheepish, back to not wanting to make eye contact. She needed him to take his sad look and go home so she could unravel her own feelings of guilt and figure out what she would tell Andrew, and when. *How the hell have I managed to mess this all up?*

Matt shuffled out the front door and began walking down the hallway to the main door, which would lead him outside. *If I know this guy,* she thought to herself, *he's going to stop at the door and give me one more look back, just like the day he left me for Ann-Marie.* So she stood and waited, wanting to see if she was right.

But he didn't. Matt got to the front door and kept on walking. Which is what she needed him to do. Keep right on walking.

Abby walked back inside and closed her front door. Walking down the hallway of her old apartment, she looked around; she had memorized the cracks in the walls from a very-much-not-at-all-up-to-code building that had been through oh-so-many earthquakes, she had pulled up the carpet to reveal gorgeous hardwood floors and redone them with care and love, and she had even made the curtains hanging from the windows to match the pillows still on the couch. She loved this place so much. She had once loved Matt so much and she had at one time had a job here that she had also loved so much.

As she made her way into the living room, she picked up the scattered remnants from just moments before, gathering up the cups of wine and the bottle. She took everything into the kitchen and stood there, smiling and letting her fingertips slide over the tile she had kept so meticulously clean in the years she lived there. As she was looking around, the front door opened and in walked Ben, two pizza boxes balanced on his head.

"Hey! Got dinner." Feeling the change in the mood, he looked around. "Where's Matt?"

Abby shot a grin at her brother. "He had to go. He said to say 'bye and enjoy dinner."

Ben's expression hinted of doubt, but he took her word for it and took the pizzas to the kitchen. "More for us. Tracey says hi and said she'd pick us up from the airport, if Ziggy isn't already."

Abby had made her way back into the living room and had plopped down on the couch. Ben joined her, two paper plates with him, both piled with a few slices each of cheese and pepperoni pizza.

"So," Ben began as he sat next to her on her old black leather couch.

"So, what?" Abby asked.

"Abs, you're killing me. What's your decision? What are you doing?"

Abby took a bite from a slice of cheese pizza and sat there for a second, her mind momentarily lapsing as she let it wander back to the heated moments with Matt. She shook them off, vowing to deal with her guilt later. She turned and focused on Ben.

"I had to go to come back, Ben." Abby grinned. "Let's go home."

Thank you for reading *Gotta Go To Come Back,* the second story in the **Abby George Series**.
I hope you enjoyed it! If you did:

- Leave a review (it helps others find this book)
- Stop by my website & sign up for my newsletter at www.annekemp.com

The other Abby George stories:
Rum Punch Regrets
Sugar City Secrets

Do you enjoy romance books set on tropical islands? Then you'll like these novellas. You'll even see some familiar faces pop up!

A Second Chance for Christmas
The Reality of Romance

Come and say hello on social media

facebook.com/missannekemp

twitter.com/MissAnneKemp

instagram.com/missannekemp

pinterest.com/annekemp

Made in the USA
Las Vegas, NV
03 January 2023

64766101R00059